# THE JORDANS MURDER

# Borgo Press Books by S. Fowler Wright

# THE JORDANS MURDER

## AN INSPECTOR COMBRIDGE AND MR. JELLIPOT CLASSIC CRIME NOVEL

by

## S. FOWLER WRIGHT

## WRITING AS "SYDNEY FOWLER"

## THE BORGO PRESS

*An Imprint of Wildside Press LLC*

**MMIX**

# CONTENTS

# THE JORDANS MURDER

# CHAPTER I.

TUCKER EMMOLL came from New Mexico. He came to London with more money to spend than most men should have, and with an introduction to the secretary of a highly respectable London club.

It was an introduction that the secretary could not ignore, for it came from one who had given lavish hospitality in New Orleans to friends of his own recommendation. Mr. Emmoll was dined at the club. Certain members of the Committee, more or less accustomed to such ordeals, entertained and endured a man whom they could not like, and plied him with wine, until the need for endurance passed, and the entertainment was theirs. For Emmoll, being in liquor, talked.

He was not quite foolish enough to give his true name, nor to narrate how he had fled across the ocean thirty-five years before from the imminent shadow of a Manchester jail. But he told tales of lawless violences in Colorado camps, in which he had taken brutal, sometimes homicidal part, which he appeared to regard as matters for boast rather than shame.

He told, at the last, a tale of how he had been knocked down by another man, also of English origin, and how quickly the insult had been avenged. He had risen with his hand already upon the six-shooter which was, if his account was to be believed, the sole authority which that community knew, but found that his opponent had been quicker than he, so that he had gazed down the muzzle of a pistol levelled within a few feet of his own eyes.

Even then, he boasted, his nerve had not failed, nor had his wit been unable to bring him through the encounter with a reputation more feared than before. He had been quick to express his regret, to admit that he had deserved what he got, and as his apology had been accepted, and his opponent's weapon sunk, he had raised his own and shot the man who was so credulous a fool as to suppose that he would forgive the insult of such a blow.

"That," he said, with a complacent chuckle creasing cheeks which had become somewhat heavy from the good living in recent years, "was the end of Jim Hartlin. Not a bad fellow at all, but a bit too quick to quarrel, and a bit too soft for the habits of Slider's Creek."

"Did you say Hartlin—Jim Hartlin?" a quiet voice asked. It was that of a man in his early fifties. A barrister who was spoken of as likely to be Attorney-General if the next election should bring his political party to power.

"Yes," Emmoll said. "I'm not one to forget a name."

"It isn't a common name."

"No, I don't say that it is. I don't say that I've met with it since. But that's what it was."

The barrister appeared to check himself on the threshold of further speech. Then he said casually: "I only thought that it was an unusual name; and of course it was a long time ago."

"So it was, but Tuck Emmoll never forgets a name," the man replied, without meeting the speaker's eyes. The incident was no more to him than a dozen others which he had told to show these ineffectual fossils what real manhood was. But after that the talk halted, and was not freely resumed.

Mr. Emmoll may have observed this, or he may have been actuated by nothing more than a prudent thought that he would leave while he could still do so on steady legs. Anyhow, he departed shortly afterwards, thanking his hosts for the hospitality he had received, and with his wits insufficiently alert to observe that more than one of them avoided shaking his hand as he retired.

After he had gone, the barrister left, accompanied by a solicitor with whom he had associations both of professional and personal kinds.

"So," he said, "I have learned at last how Jim Hartlin died."

"He was your cousin?"

"Yes. He was also my dearest friend."

The solicitor made no answer. After a pause, his companion went on: "When you think that a swine like that can thrive, while better men—" He broke off abruptly, and then added: "I should enjoy killing him with my own hands!"

He spoke with a bitterness which caused the solicitor to look mildly surprised. He answered reasonably "I suppose there must be many who feel like that. The trouble is that the man who kills another, however much he may deserve it, usually bas a worse time than the man he killed."

"Usually, not always. I don't need to tell you that most violent criminals are half-witted, which makes the work of detection about twice as easy as it would otherwise be. If a murder should be deliberately planned and committed, say by you or me, with all the caution and forethought that we are accustomed to use in our professional work, it might be a different matter."

The solicitor considered this, but was dubious in his reply: "Perhaps so; but was doubt whether it would work out very well for us. We should think of all the precautions we could, and a good detective, if he should begin to suspect us at all, would anticipate that we should have done so. His mind would move along the same lines, and the more carefully we had planned to divert suspicion from ourselves, the more easily he might reconstruct the crime."

"Yes," the barrister replied, "that's an idea. I should say that's a sound idea...which doesn't alter the fact that there's a murderous guzzling swine alive in London tonight who won't get what he deserves, unless a better man be prepared to risk his life in a good cause."

"Yes. I see how you feel. I daresay he's got a good many enemies. You must hope that there's one with less judgment and self-restraint than your own, who'll give him something he ought to have." As he said this, they came to the entrance of the barrister's chambers, and the solicitor called a taxi for his own use.

# CHAPTER II.

EZRA BECKWITH, being conscious of advancing years, and a very troublesome cough, decided to make a will. He therefore wrote to his solicitor, Mr. Jellipot, asking him to visit him during the coming weekend to discuss the matter.

Mr. Beckwith lived at Seer Green, which is a pleasant village in the neighbourhood of the Chalfonts, about twenty-five miles from London. Mr. Jellipot, knowing his client to be a man of leisurely and discursive mind, surmised correctly that the document would not be completed without prolonged discussion, and replied that he would come on Saturday afternoon and return on Monday. Mr. Beckwith having responded suitably, Mr. Jellipot came.

Jellipot took an early walk at sunrise on Sunday morning, in the direction of Jordans, which he knew by repute as the burial-place of William Penn and other Quaker celebrities, but had not previously visited.

Mr. Jellipot had continued a rather embarrassing discussion upon the terms of the proposed will until a late hour of the previous night. At that time his elderly client had suggested that they should meet again at breakfast, which he had ordered for 10:00 A.M., saying that Mr. Jellipot would be glad of a good night after his legal labours during the week.

Mr. Jellipot had been too polite to reply that he preferred to breakfast at an earlier hour. But he was a man of fixed habits, and at 7:00 A.M., feeling his usual inclination to rise, he decided to visit the famous graveyard, if opportunity should allow. He saw that he would have ample time to do this, and to return before breakfast would be served. So, having dressed, he went out through a silent house.

His walk lay through green undulating country, moderately wooded and sprinkled with the pleasant, unpretentious dwellings of London business men. He admired it absently, but he was already familiar with the general characteristics of the scenery of the Chiltern Hills, and his mind was inclined to dwell upon the will which would be his task to draw up.

Yet he was sufficiently conscious of outward things not to overlook the purpose for which he came. When he reached the Meeting-House beside which the founder of Pennsylvania lies in the quiet dignity of his turf-clad grave, he turned into the field-like burial-ground, beautiful in its ancient simplicity, with a thought that, if all men were of the disposition of those who lay buried there, the world would become a fairer and better place.

He continued his walk, musing. Here, in this peaceful place, which seemed quietly alive with a better spirit than that which stirred men of violence to crime and feud.... Mr. Jellipot stopped abruptly, gazing at a most shocking, monstrous, and impossible thing.

The centre of Jordans consists of a group of houses surrounding a village green, the approach to which is a broad semi-private avenue, leading off from the main road, and lying on the left hand as it was passed by Mr. Jellipot.

Farther on, there are footpaths also approaching the green at different points. One of these paths is entered by a stile, slightly raised from the footpath level, and constructed of two uprights, two cross-bars, and a flat plank crossing the lower bar at a slant, for the convenience of those whose legs are too short or stiff to mount it conveniently without this assisting step.

Mr. Jellipot might have passed this stile with no more attention than it deserved, had it been vacant, or ornamented only by a living person normally clothed. But the figure that met his gaze was naked, grotesquely postured, and quite certainly dead. Mr. Jellipot paused abruptly, gazed incredulously, and approached the apparition with a greater inclination to disbelieve his own eyes than he would have thought it possible to experience in his waking hours.

Closer inspection added detail, which did not dispel the marvel, nor make it less. Mr. Jellipot, puzzled at his own reaction, and analytic of mind, as his habit was, thought: "If it were less fantastically impossible, it would be more horrible than it is."

He looked on the body of a man, who had passed his youth, and, though still muscular, had become somewhat obese. His legs, before death or after, had been pushed through the stile, so that they rested upon the lower bar, and his heels were on the ground that sloped down from the stile to the road level. His body was seated on the cross-plank, and his head and arms hung forward over the upper bar. The general effect was that of a man set in the stocks.

If he had come to a violent end, which was easy to think, its cause was not evident at a first view, unless it could be attributed to a penknife, the blade of which had been driven into his navel, so that only the small pearl-sided sheath projected therefrom.

Considering what he saw with a mind now widely alert, and convinced that he had come upon the result of bizarre crime or a madman's end, he reflected that the blade of the penknife could not be longer than the exposed sheath into which it must have closed. If that were so, it could not have inflicted a fatal wound. He observed that no bleeding had followed its insertion, and concluded that it must have been driven in some time after death had occurred. That might seem a small fact in itself, but it definitely indicated murder rather than suicide. Mr. Jellipot was not one to allow himself to be hurried in his conclusions, but he recognized it to be a matter with which the police should be promptly acquainted.

He looked round at a few houses scattered along the sides of the road, hurried to the nearest one and knocked on the door. A thin, elderly woman appeared, with a hand on the open door, waiting silently for Mr. Jellipot to explain his presence.

"I'm sorry to have to tell you," he said, "that there's been a—an accident up the road. There's a man dead."

"The roads aren't safe for anyone these days. You never know who it'll be next," said the woman.

15

"I don't think it's a motor accident," Mr. Jellipot replied. "It's a matter," he went on, "about which the police ought to be informed at once, but I don't think it—he ought to be left as he is. I suppose you haven't got a telephone here?"

"No, you'd find one at Miss Mendip's. That's the house with the white gate, down the road."

"Yes?" Jellipot answered doubtfully. "I suppose there isn't any man about here that I can ask—or," with a sudden inspiration, "if you could lend me a sheet?"

"Yes, I could do that," she answered. "I'd better get George, my lodger, to come." She raised her voice slightly to call: "George," and a young man appeared at once from an inner room, wiping a full mouth.

George was stolid and large. He listened to Mr. Jellipot's severely restricted statement of the presence of a murdered man at the stile without visible emotion. Then he went with a slow but willing heaviness to bring the sheet from the double bed, as his landlady asked him to do.

The next moment George appeared with a clean sheet loosely folded over his arm, and walked at Jellipot's side the short distance to the stile without indulging in further speech.

His eyes became somewhat rounded at the sight of the grotesque posture and nudity of the murdered man. "Looks," he said laconically, "as though they crocked him to swipe his duds."

"It is," Jellipot admitted, "a possible but still inadequate explanation."

George, who had come from London three months before, when he had obtained a position as assistant to a Seer Green butcher, surveyed the dead body with the professional interest of a licensed slaughter-man. He looked under the sagging chin. "Been bled," he explained, with the finality of one who knew; "bled slow." He looked on the ground, and added: "I'm satisfied that it wasn't done here. Wonder how they lugged him along."

"I suppose," Jellipot said reasonably, "that it must have been brought by car." He was unaware of George's professional qualifications, but recognized the tone of authority with which he spoke. He asked: "How long should you say he's been dead?"

"Might be a day, or perhaps two. You couldn't say nearer than that." Together they draped the sheet over the unseemly spectacle. "I wonder," Jellipot said, "that no one noticed this before I came along—that is, if it was put here during the night, as I suppose."

"Folks aren't over-early on Sundays round here. Not as I've seen. There'd be the milkman. He must have come by."

"It seems scarcely possible that the milkman would not have observed it, if it were here when he passed."

"Don't know that I'd say that. Driving on a road he knows, and not much light at that hour."

"I expect you are right," Jellipot allowed, realizing that George's judgment was supported by the apparent fact. He proposed that he should telephone the police, while George would remain on guard till their arrival.

Jellipot, becoming aware that he would be late for a breakfast that he was beginning to need, set off briskly in search of Miss Mendip's telephone.

# CHAPTER III.

MR. JELLIPOT had further occasion to observe that the inhabitants of Jordans do not rise early on Sunday mornings during the winter months, while he pressed Miss Mendip's bell at reasonable intervals for four or five minutes. Finally a maid appeared and looked at him in a vacuous silence through the narrow gap of a quarter-opened door.

"Would you please ask Mendip if she would kindly allow me to use her telephone for a few minutes?" Mr. Jellipot inquired, and then added, as the girl still regarded him with dull eyes and a slack jaw: "I am sorry to trouble you at this early hour, but it is a matter of urgency. There has been a—an accident up the road."

"If you'll come this way, sir, if you please," said the girl, and led him upstairs to a bedroom from which its recent occupant had withdrawn.

"I want," he said, when he had picked up the receiver, and heard the operator's response, "to be put through to the nearest police station at once."

The call went through swiftly.

"Inspector Dutton speaking."

"There is a man murdered," Jellipot replied, "at the side of the road at Jordans, about a quarter of a mile from the Meeting-House."

"Why do you say murdered?"

"Because it is obvious that he has died from violence, and there are evidences that it has not been self-inflicted. The man is quite naked, and has been fixed on a stile at the side of the road."

*"Naked?"*

"Yes."

"Who are you?"

"My name is Jellipot. I am a London solicitor. I am staying for the weekend at the house of a client, Mr. Beckwith, at Seer Green."

The information slightly diminished the curtness of the next query, but there was still a sharp doubt in the inspector's voice. "Where are you speaking from?"

"In view of the urgency of the matter, I have asked for the use of the telephone of a neighbouring resident."

"Name of?"

"Miss Mendip, I understand."

"Body been interfered with in any way?"

"No. A sheet has been put over it, and a young man named George, who lives near, has kindly undertaken to stay there till you arrive."

"Sure it isn't a car accident?"

"Yes, quite."

"I'll be there in ten minutes. Of course you'll wait till I come."

"I'm afraid not. I was taking a walk before breakfast, which I have not yet had, when I made this discovery. I am going back to get some."

"All the same, I must ask you to stay till I arrive. Miss Mendip will give you something, if you ask her. Or anyone else in Jordans. You'll find they're quite hospitable."

"All the same, I must decline. I have an appointment to breakfast with my host. You can get in touch with me at Mr. Beckwith's any time during the day, but I have already given you all the help I can."

Mr. Jellipot might have said more had he not become conscious that Inspector Dutton had rung off. That competent officer had understood that Mr. Jellipot meant what he said, and had wasted no further time in requesting that which he had no power to enforce.

Mr. Jellipot saw that if his meal were not to be further delayed it would be necessary to go before the police-inspector should arrive, and he rightly concluded that the interval would not be long.

Seven minutes later, Inspector Dutton arrived in a car from which a sergeant and two constables emerged after himself. He would have picked up the police-surgeon also but for a lurking fear that the telephone message he had received was no more than a practical joke.

A few words with George, and the sight of the sheeted stile, were sufficient to convince him that he was faced by no hoax, but one of those spectacular crimes which draw a whole nation's eyes as they become known, as this must do in the space of a few hours.

"Jones," he said, "phone Doctor Cartlidge to come at once. There's a house with a phone over there. Yes, Mendip's the name. Then phone for the Beaconsfield ambulance. No. The stretcher at St. Giles wouldn't do it. They must rush the ambulance here at once. We can't leave this here. There'll be the people coming along to church in less than an hour now. No, Bellis, leave the sheet as it is till Doctor Cartlidge comes. Here, come back, I haven't finished with you yet."

The last words were addressed to George, who had shown an inclination to retire modestly from the scene. He was to experience the diluted suspicion which spreads like a diffused light around those who are found by the police in the neighbourhood of a violent crime.

Dr. Cartlidge's car and the Beaconsfield ambulance arrived almost at the same moment. The two vehicles, by Inspector Dutton's order, were drawn close to the side of the road, partially screening the stile from the general view. This may have been well, in the interests of public propriety, concerning which Inspector Dutton felt a vague responsibility, but Dr. Cartlidge cared not at all.

"Take it off!" he said. "Do you think I can see through a linen sheet? Um! Dead enough now, and dead enough I should say when he was brought here." He looked at the protruding penknife without attempting to touch it. "Queer idea of a joke," he said. And then to Inspector Dutton: "Any lunatic at large round these parts?"

"No. I don't know that there is. This looks to me like the work of more than one man."

"Perhaps it is. But a madman's frenzy, you know! Wonderful what they can do." He was examining the puncture under the chin as he spoke. He looked up at George "You the one who was found with him?" he asked sharply.

Inspector Dutton, a just though sceptical man, would have explained, but the doctor went on rapidly: "You're the man who came to me from Seer Green with a poisoned finger, aren't you?"

"Yes, sir. But it's quite well now, sir. Thanks to you, sir, it is."

George's tone was propitiatory, but the doctor went on: "You're the new slaughter-man at Bennett's, aren't you?"

"Yes, sir. That's me."

The doctor's eyes went back to that small, deep wound through which a man's life had been drained away. But he only added: "Well, it was a neat job," and shut his mouth on the words.

"I'm glad," he said to Dutton, "you thought of the ambulance. I think the best way would be to get him away, stile and all. I can't do anything here."

Inspector Dutton did not object. He wanted that unseemly object removed as soon as possible from the eyes of the Jordans children. He said: "Well, if we borrow a good saw— Bellis, see what you can do. Jones, keep those people back. Tell them to clear, or I'll run some of them in. I daresay they know a lot more about this than they'll be willing to tell. What's that car stopping for? Tell them to move on, or they'll get a summons for blocking the road."

The voice of authority, sharply urged, made a partial clearance of the lane, which had been gradually filling up with a larger and closer crowd. A collection of three saws enabled a start to be made in the removal of the stile from its too-firm foundations. Half an hour later the ambulance moved away at a walking pace, lest it should jolt its ghastly freight. After that the crowd gradually scattered to talk and wonder, while P. C. Bellis took a stolid stand by the shortened posts of the stile.

# CHAPTER IV.

MR JELLIPOT was no more than twenty minutes late for the breakfast hour which his host had mentioned the night before. Though Mr. Beckwith had waited for him, with a courtesy which some elderly gentlemen might not have exercised after being told that their guest had left the house without explanation two or three hours earlier, Mr. Jellipot felt that the exceptional narrative which he had to offer should be a sufficient apology.

When the meal was done, he accepted a proposal that he should retire to Mr. Beckwith's study, both to draft the body of the proposed will, and to prepare a schedule of charities which it would be intended to benefit, for his client's final approval. Having done this in the course of the following hour, he turned his thoughts again to consideration of the unusual spectacle of the morning hours.

He sat for over half an hour in motionless thought, debating a point upon which he found himself to be in an indecision very difficult to resolve. Then he reached for the telephone, and put through a call to Detective Inspector Combridge.

"That you, Combridge?" he said, as he heard a familiar voice at the other end of the wire. "Jellipot speaking. I'm at Seer Green. I suppose you know where that is. Yes, staying here for the weekend. But I've not called you to tell you that. You remember doing me a good turn once, when you brought Ada Hamilton in to see me? Well, it's my turn now. There's been rather an odd murder committed here. At least this is where they've dumped the body. It's a case where they'll be certain to call in the Yard. I thought you might like to be at hand to take up the case."

This information was received with five seconds' silence before a reply came, with no enthusiasm in the inspector's voice. "It's good of you to ring me up. But I'm not sure that six days a week isn't as much as I feel called on to do, unless they come after me."

"It is a point of view," Mr. Jellipot replied readily, "with which it is easy to sympathize." He would have hung up with no further remarks beyond those that courtesy required, had he not heard, in a curiously altered voice:

"But if you've learned anything on the spot, you might give me a few tips, all the same. If I do get put on it, it'll save time, and you may know something I couldn't get from the local police."

"No. I can't claim any special knowledge. I happened to take an early morning walk and saw a dead man with his head hanging over a tile, and his arms and legs stuck through it, and I just put the police on and came away."

"Sure he was murdered?"

"I was assured by George, which is the name of a young man who spoke in a professional tone, that he must have been bled slowly to death, and as that had not occurred at the spot where he was, he must have been taken there later. It may not follow that he was murdered, but you will agree that it is a probable deduction.

"What sort of a man was he?"

"Middle-aged. Rather heavy. The sort who would probably call himself a gentleman, though the opinion might not be unanimously sustained."

"Yes. I see. But—was he the sort who might have been murdered for what he had on him, or one more likely to get killed in a row—racing-gangster type? You know what I mean."

"He hadn't anything on him whatever."

"You don't mean that literally? You mean they'd picked his pockets? It doesn't sound a particularly odd murder to me. Commonplace is the word I should use. But I suppose coming on it as you did—"

"I mean literally. He was quite naked. No clothes at all."

"That was certainly odd. Sorry I didn't appreciate it before. Anything else you can tell me I shall be glad to hear, and I won't interrupt again."

"I'm afraid there's no more to tell, except that Police-Inspector Dutton has been waiting in the hall for the last ten minutes."

"Never mind him. What's your address if I come down?" Jellipot gave this information, added that he was leaving by an early train on the following morning, and hung up the receiver.

\* \* \* \* \* \* \*

Mr. Jellipot's work for the day was done. He had agreed with Mr. Beckwith that the will could not be completed without inquiries concerning the exact designations and activities of some of the charities which it was intended to benefit, and that it would be necessary for him to pay a second visit to Jordans on the following weekend for his client to approve and sign it. On this understanding, Mr. Beckwith retired immediately after an early dinner, as it was his custom to do, and Mr. Jellipot was left to indulge himself with the resources of an excellent library, or his own thoughts, as he might prefer.

He sat for a long time in apparent idleness while his mind reviewed the experience of the morning, and speculated upon its probable developments. Once he said aloud: "It has the appearance of a most unlikely coincidence." And then, more firmly, as though the cool sanity of his mind regained its control "Such coincidences do not occur."

Yet, he asked himself, if coincidence must be eliminated, what conclusion remained? It seemed that he built a superstructure of conjecture upon one tiny fact (if fact it could be called) grotesquely inadequate for the foundation of such an edifice. "Well," he said, after a further interval, "Combridge is a sound man." But there was neither confidence nor satisfaction in the tone in which these words were spoken, and he still sat silent and absorbed in his own thoughts, until he was roused by the information that Chief Inspector Combridge was in the hall, and had asked to see him.

24

"Show him in please, Edith," he said, and received him, when he appeared, with his usual cordiality. "You've not been long," he said, "in getting on the job."

"No," Inspector Combridge answered readily, "we don't loose much time in getting to work in such cases as this, and I've got to thank you that I was on the ground when I was. When I reached the Yard, I found that Davis had just tried to phone me. You must have saved me an hour."

"Then," Mr. Jellipot calculated, "you've been down here four or five hours already."

"Yes. About that."

"If you feel that the hint which I was able to give you, and our past acquaintance, justify me in asking, I shall be interested to know what progress you have made, and to hear your theory of what appears to me to be a most puzzling crime."

"Well," Inspector Combridge replied, "I came to learn what I could from you, rather than to tell you what we've been able to find; but I've no more that can be done before morning. And there's nothing I mind telling you—also I'd like to learn any ideas you may have about what certainly is, in some aspects, a puzzling case."

Mr. Jellipot smiled. "I can't remember," he said, "in the Hamilton case, that you gave any help to me."

"I don't remember that you needed much either. This is an altogether different position. We're both law-abiding citizens discussing how a particularly brutal and offensive murderer—or perhaps I should say murderers, as it could hardly have been done by one man—should be caught and hanged. You've got a wonderful faculty for thinking these things out, and, if you can help me with any ideas, you know whether we should fall out over that."

"Yes," Mr. Jellipot admitted, "I'm sure we shouldn't, though you may easily overrate my capacity. I suppose there may be difficulty in finding a natural explanation for some of the less usual circumstances of the murder. Why, for instance, had the murdered man been completely stripped? Was it done before or after death? Was the idea to render his identification more difficult?"

"I shouldn't say it was that," the inspector answered, concentrating his reply upon the last question, which had been the subject of some debate with the local officers just before he had set out on his present visit.

"It seems inconsistent, for one thing, with the conspicuous way in which the body was set up. But if you say that that argument isn't sound, it still remains that it was an almost crazy thing to have done.

"In the first place, the clothes have got to be disposed of somehow or other—which isn't an easy thing to do so that no traces remain—and there's no simpler method than leaving them on the body to which they belong. As it is, they're very likely to be a clue that will lead us just where we want to get.

"And in the second, I don't suppose their removal will cause any material difficulty in identification, or even delay."

"You think you know who the dead man was?"

"Not yet, but we soon shall. We know that he was an American who had lived a hard life, but become wealthy in recent years, and tomorrow we shall have his photograph in about twenty million newspapers here, and being copied, if necessary, into as many in his own country. How many wealthy Americans do you suppose will have disappeared in the last forty-eight hours? And how could such a man disappear suddenly without a number of those around him— apart from his immediate friends or foes—observing that he wasn't there?"

"I could imagine circumstances," Mr. Jellipot replied with some hesitation, "but I see the force of your argument, and having found out so much, I should think your confidence is well grounded that you will soon know who he was. May I ask how his nationality, and the other circumstances you mention, can be so definitely deduced?"

"He wore a dental plate that had been made in the United States or Canada, and his mouth showed other evidences of American dentistry."

"And as to his wealth, and earlier conditions of life?"

"He was originally a powerful, muscular man and his body, though it had become flabby and overfed, had many evidences of rough living. A wound of some kind—probably from a knife-thrust—had grazed his ribs. You may have noticed that?"

"No. I can't say I did. I was less concerned to study the—the exhibit—than to arrange for it to be covered or removed."

"That was natural enough. But the scar was there. And there's another on his left hip, where he must have been shot from behind. Then there are signs of an old blow over the head that must have nearly fractured his skull. When you add that the top joint of one fingers gone, you may conclude that he's come through some lively times."

"But that hardly shows that he had become wealthy before he died."

"No. But when you find that such a man has come to grow a big paunch and has manicured hands? Hands that still show the rough uses they had for thirty or forty years, which no manicuring can altogether remove? And when you find that he's actually had his feet manicured too?"

"Pedicured," Mr. Jellipot suggested gently, "might be the more orthodox word," but beyond this correction of his visitor's less accurate vocabulary, he offered no dissent from the conclusions to which he had listened.

"I don't mind what you call it so that you know what I mean," the inspector replied with momentary irritation. "When we've had the post mortem and learn what he's like inside, we shall know a lot more than we do now."

"I have no doubt that you will. Your methods have a thoroughness which it is impossible not to admire. Any fingerprints anywhere? I suppose they wouldn't show—or would they?—on the body or on the stile?"

"There aren't any. Even the penknife handle hadn't a trace. It must have been held in a covered hand, or wiped after it was put in."

"I thought the fact that the knife was left, and the way in which it had been inserted in the dead body, were about the oddest parts of the crime."

"So it looked to me, though I suppose it was no more than the impulse of a man who had lost his mental balance from what he'd

27

done already. Doctor Cartlidge says it appears to be the same weapon, small as it is, with which the murder was done."

"Then you regard it as the work of a single man?"

"I didn't say that. He'd have to be one of most exceptional strength. The murdered man wasn't a lightweight. I should say it was almost certainly the work of a gang, and probably done as it was for a warning to others who would be sure to hear of it, and understand."

"It is at least a plausible theory," Mr. Jellipot considered, "and it's evident that where large sums of money are handled, or where the possibility of betrayal arises, among men of unscrupulous character, and for whom the protection of the law does not apply, the discipline of violence is the only one by which their leaders can restrain them. By the way, Inspector Dutton appeared to look with suspicion upon a young man who was introduced to me by the name of George, and whom I was instrumental in bringing upon the scene. I should be interested to know whether you've found reason to incline to the same view."

"No, I shouldn't like to say that, not beyond the degree to which we're suspicious of everyone till we find some positive reason to rule them out. He isn't a native here. He came from London a few months ago. We'll check up on that, and find out what his record is I'm told that he answered an advertisement for a slaughter-man by a local butcher. He hasn't an alibi, as he happens to sleep in a ground-floor room which he could leave during the night without anyone knowing. But that's a long way from saying he did it. His character's quite good locally. There's just the fact of his being on the scene, and I understand that's due to you."

"Yes. Entirely so. It would be unjust to put that against him in any way."

"So I understood. Apart from that, there's only the way the man was killed, which would be more likely to occur to a pork-butcher than the average murderer. I suppose you haven't any reason to suspect him yourself?"

"Not the least. I'm just interested to learn."

"Well, that's how it is. But I wish you'd tell me what happened this morning more fully than you did on the telephone. I heard it from Dutton since, but I'd rather have it from you direct."

Mr. Jellipot made no objection to this request, and the conversation continued until a late hour, but without settling upon any fact not already recorded, or any theory of more than a vaguely plausible kind.

# CHAPTER V.

WITH the unspectacular thoroughness that characterizes the highly organized modern methods of detecting crime, the investigation proceeded, and bore its first fruits on Tuesday morning. At that time the avid appetite of the public was fed, if not satisfied, with the information that the body of the murdered man had been identified as that of James Tucker Emmoll, commonly known as Tuck Emmoll, a wealthy American, who had checked out of a London hotel and had forwarded his luggage to Southampton on the previous Friday, but had failed to board the liner by which he should have sailed on the following day.

With this expected success, Inspector Combridge felt that the path of investigation was opening smoothly before him. If the murderers of Tucker Emmoll have the means of identification when they stripped the body, they must have had a lesson, as they opened the Tuesday morning newspapers, of the futility of plans which are intended to flout the law.

Certainly, they had not destroyed the clothes; nor had they endeavoured to rid themselves of them in such a manner that they would be likely to remain undiscovered for any prolonged period. The news came in by telephone from the High Wycombe police that two boys, going to school by a path that led over one of the bare green uplands that are characteristic of the higher Chilterns, had come upon a neatly folded pile of clothes, somewhat sodden with morning rain. On top of the clothes was an envelope, addressed to Chief Inspector Combridge. Within this envelope was a sheet of

white notepaper, on which was written a stanza of presumably original verse:

> *Sought the brute, and caught the brute,*
> *(And thank you kindly, ma'am),*
> *Brought the brute, and taught the brute,*
> *For that's the kind I am.*
> *Tight again by night again,*
> *And never cared a damn.*

This information came to Inspector Combridge by telephone,
and. cheeky as it appeared to be, it did nothing to depress his spirits.

"Well," he said to his informant at the High Wycombe police
station, "that ought to land us a day's march nearer home, as the
hymn says. But I must get off to the inquest now. No, we shan't
want it for that today. In fact, I shan't want it to get known to the
public at all at present. We'd better leave the scoundrels guessing
whether it's been found, or what we make of it, if it has. Do you
think you can keep it out of the newspapers? Well, do the best you
can. I'll be with you as soon as the inquest's adjourned, and that
shouldn't take more than couple of hours."

He spoke with knowledge of what to expect, and, in fact, it took
less time than that. For when he arrived on the scene of inquiry Inspector Dutton was already giving evidence of the finding and removal of the murdered body. After that Mr. Jellipot narrated its discovery, and the steps he took to inform the police, and to insure that
the more youthful eyes of the peaceful Quaker community should
not be contaminated by such a sight. His account was accepted with
brevity, and was not questioned in any particular. George Tipper
was not called

Dr. Cartlidge said there could be no doubt that the man had bled
to death through a wound in the throat which might have been, and
almost certainly had been, inflicted with the penknife which was
found inserted in a lower part of the body. The presence of the knife
in that position made it almost certain that the man had not died by
his own hand, but it was a curious fact that there was no indication

that any struggle had preceded the murder. There were no minor injuries. No bruises. No signs that the man's hands or feet had been bound before he had been executed in such a manner.

"Which," the coroner commented, "suggests an anaesthetic?"

"Yes."

"But there was no sign of such having been used?"

"No. None at all. I shouldn't say that is conclusive; but there had certainly been no hypodermic injection."

He went on to describe the contents of the stomach, which indicated that death had occurred about four hours after a meal had been taken.

He was followed on the witness stand by a hotel porter who definitely identified the body as that of Mr. Tucker Emmoll, whom he had seen alive and well, jovial and properly clothed, on the Friday night before Mr. Jellipot had discovered it in a condition of unseemly nudity, grotesquely lolling upon the Jordans stile.

Having taken this evidence, the coroner said briefly that as the inquiry was in the hands of the police, he saw no advantage in carrying it beyond the point already reached. He then adjourned it sine die, leaving the public appetite stimulated rather than satisfied by the slight additional lifting of the curtain of homicidal drama, and without mention of the neatly folded, rain-sodden heap of clothes which had been placed during the previous night on the treeless High Wycombe hill.

Combridge returned to his office just in time to receive a phone call from Jellipot.

"The character of Jordans village," Mr. Jellipot said, "so far as my limited opportunities have enabled me to assess it, is friendly, peaceful, and discreet. It's difficult to imagine a community less likely to be associated, however indirectly, with Emmoll's murder. But gossip there is certain to be. There's a lady—doubtless of excellent reputation—a Miss Manly, a member of the Management Committee by which the affairs of the village are controlled. Miss Prudence Manly. It may lead to nothing, and I am sure you will respect my wish that I should not be mentioned as the source from which the suggestion comes. You might ask her if there may be any information bearing upon the crime which she is able to give."

"You'd rather not say more than that?"

"No. In fact," Mr. Jellipot added with increased animation, "I would rather have said less."

Inspector Combridge did not interview Miss Manly quite as promptly as he had expected to do. He found on inquiry that she was away for the weekend and was expected home on Tuesday morning. Besides, other developments had occurred which required his immediate attention and were of a more definitely promising kind.

The first of these was the discovery of the man who had driven Emmoll from the hotel. The explanation of his delayed appearance was simply that he had been away on a short holiday. He had spent a week in Paris, and, on reading the police circular when he returned, he had driven at once to Scotland Yard to report that he had picked up such a fare on the night in question. He explained that he had left the man at the Savoy, where he had seen him shake hands with another gentleman, whom he described rather vaguely but thought he would recognize if he should see him again.

And the value of this information was almost immediately discounted—except as needless corroboration—through a letter which came to Inspector Combridge by the midday delivery:

*Dear Sir,*

*Re: Tucker Emmoll*

*If you can call at my once today at any time between 4:00 and 6:00 A.M., I shall be able to give you some information concerning the movements of the above during the earlier hours of the night on which his murder occurred.*

*Yours faithfully,*

*Denis Hartlin*

It was punctually at four o'clock that the inspector called at Mr. Hartlin's offices in the Inner Temple, and found himself shown without delay into the room where the barrister was accustomed to give conferences to his clients.

Mr. Hartlin was a man of a lean muscularity, physically and intellectually alert, black of hair, and rather sallow-skinned, with very bright dark eyes that could intimidate a witness or woo a jury with equal ease and success.

He was an able advocate, both in civil and criminal causes, sound in law and subtle of wit, but his greatest asset may have been his voice. Now he received his visitor with a quiet cordiality. "Sit down, Inspector," he said. "I don't know that what I'm going to tell you will be very much use—you must judge that for yourself—but I feel that I owe you some apology for not having let you know earlier.

"The fact is that I was so closely engaged all last week on the Astill case that I didn't give the newspapers even a glance till it was finished on Friday night. I knew about the murder, of course. I'd read that during the previous weekend, and I believe I heard some talk subsequently about the body having been identified, but I wasn't particularly interested, being fully occupied, as I have said, with one of the most complicated cases which I have ever had to handle. The thought that the murdered man might be Tucker Emmoll never entered my mind.

"But I looked at one of the Sunday newspapers yesterday, and read that man's name, and that you were hunting for the taxi-driver who picked him up at the hotel. I can't give you the taxi-driver's name, but I can tell you something that makes it unimportant. Tucker Emmoll was driven to the Savoy, where he was dining with me on my invitation."

"Well," the inspector answered, "that certainly gets us a step forward; but what I shall be most anxious to know is where he went when he left you. If you can tell me that, we ought to be getting warm, for, by the medical evidence, within four hours of eating that dinner he was a dead man."

"Well, more or less, I can do that, though I can't say how much it will be. He told me he was going to Southampton by car—I don't know that that's of any importance, as it seems he didn't go—but before that he wanted to say good-bye to a friend. As I had my car there and was going in the same direction, I gave him a lift and put him down at the south end of Marsden Terrace."

Hearing this, Inspector Combridge realized that he would not go back to the office to report that he had drawn in no more than an empty net. It was, in fact, not the first time that he had heard the name of Marsden Terrace in the course of his inquiries concerning the movements and associations of the dead man. He asked: "I suppose you don't know the address any nearer than that?"

"No. But my chauffeur thinks he does. He's not definite, and you may prefer to question him rather than take a hearsay from me. But I may explain that it was at Emmoll's own request that I dropped him at the end of the road instead of taking him to the door, and when I told Blake to do that he asked which end of Marsden Terrace he meant—it's rather long as you probably know—and Emmoll didn't know London well enough to say north or south. So he mentioned the number of the house to which he was going, thinking that might be an indication, as in fact it was, for Blake, who knows more of London than I know of the law, says the numbers in that part of the West End all run the same way."

"It wasn't anything in the Forties?"

"Yes. I believe it was."

"Then I think I know it. But I'll have a word with your man all the same. You never know where you'll pick up something that helps. I suppose he didn't let anything out during dinner that might be a pointer to what happened during the night?"

"No. I can't say he did."

Feeling that there was no more to be learned here, Inspector Combridge got up to go. He had been frank to a point, yet economical of his own knowledge, which was a matter of habit rather than design. He had little doubt that he could walk straight to the door which had admitted Tucker Emmoll after he left Denis Hartlin's car, for he had not only that almost certain guess as to the identity of the

35

woman on whom Emmoll called; he had the knowledge of that foolish stanza, which he had not mentioned to the barrister, and which connected her with the murder itself in a way that would at least justify close questioning.

He paused at the sight of a dark-blue car, unostentatiously expensive, which stood at the curb opposite to the entrance of the barrister's offices. He spoke to the chauffeur, who was sitting impassively at the wheel without appearing to regard his presence, even when he stepped up to the door.

"I suppose," he said, "this is Mr. Hartlin's car?"

The man, being directly addressed, turned his face, and answered civilly: "Yes, sir. Mr. Denis Hartlin's car."

"I am Chief Inspector Combridge," he said, coming to the point directly. "I understand from Mr. Hartlin that you drove Tucker Emmoll to Marsden Terrace on the night he was murdered. He said that you might possibly be able to tell me something helpful."

Blake opened the door of the car and invited the inspector to take the seat beside him. "There's no need to stand," he said easily, "though there isn't very much I can tell, and whether it's any use is for you to judge.

"Mr. Hartlin told me to be at the Savoy at 10:00 P.M. that night and wait for him till he came out. When he did—it must have been about 10:15—he had a gentleman with him. He said: 'This gentleman's going to make a call in Marsden Terrace. I want you to go round that way and drop him at the end of the road,' or something like that. I asked which end he meant, and he wasn't clear, not knowing London well, but he gave me the number of the house he wanted—No. 46, I believe it was. I didn't attach any importance to it then, except as indicating the end of the road to which he wanted to get."

"I expect that was it," Inspector Combridge replied, and only his habit of reticence prevented him from adding that it was the number he had already had in his own mind. He saw that it not only made it practically certain that Tucker Emmoll had called that night on a lady who had emphatically denied that she had seen him since the previous week; it also confirmed both the accuracy of Blake's memory, and the good faith of the tale he told. But he showed no sign of this judgment, seeking to put the man on his own defence, as he added: "Still it sounds a bit queer that he should make a point of being put down at the end of the road, and at the same time be so free with the number of the house he wanted."

"Well, he made no bones about that, or the reason either. He said the lady was too particular about her reputation to like him to drive up to the door."

Inspector Combridge considered the resident who lived at No. 46 whom he had questioned with some severity three days before, and was now evidently going to question again in a grimmer manner. Marie Le Noir, as she called herself, or Minnie Black, as she was known to the police, belonged to a profession for which he had no respect, even when it was carried on with a discretion which had kept clear of the criminal law.

"And after that you drove Mr. Hartlin home?"

"Yes. We got back within ten minutes from then."

"And I suppose I needn't ask whether you saw or heard anything further of Tucker Emmoll?"

"Not till I heard you'd identified him as the murdered man." Inspector Combridge did not doubt that he heard the truth, but brought a new circumstance, slightly puzzling, to his notice. He asked: "When did you hear that?"

"When it came out in the papers last Tuesday."

"Then why didn't you let me know all this before now?"

Blake answered without appearing to notice the sharpness with which the question was put: "Perhaps I should have, but it was Mr. Hartlin's matter rather than mine, and I'd no reason to think you hadn't heard it from him."

"Hadn't you talked to him about it at all?"

"When Mr. Hartlin's got a case on like he had last week, he just gives orders; he doesn't chat."

"How many other people have you talked to about this?"

"I haven't spoken a word. I don't talk about what happens when I'm on duty unless I'm asked, as I am now, by someone who's got a right to know."

Inspector Combridge got out of the car, said good night, and boarded a passing bus with determination to interview Miss Minnie Black at once. There should be no lack of official curtness with her!

\* \* \* \* \* \* \*

On the way to Marsden Terrace, Inspector Combridge recalled the incident of his previous visit to Miss Le Noir's flat, which was the first floor of No. 46. He remembered that the street door had been opened by a woman who came up from the basement, and whom he had judged to be caretaker of the house or an attendant upon more than one of its joint occupants. He had observed that she spoke with a foreign accent, and had given a nervous start on first seeing him, a reaction familiar to his profession from those who wished to avoid unpleasant contacts with the police. A woman of good conscience would most probably not have suspected that he was a police officer, or would have been indifferent if she had.

He was pleased therefore when her face appeared at the open door, and no less because he saw it to be a pleasure she did not share. He looked at her with a disconcerting intentness, as he asked curtly: "Miss Black in?"

The woman hesitated, as though disposed to deny knowledge of the name he used, lost courage for that, and said: "If you'll take a seat for a moment, I'll see whether Miss Le Noir's in."

"You needn't do that," he answered, without moving towards the hall-chair she indicated "You know she's in. *I hope you haven't forgotten to register lately?*"

It was a bold and random shot, but he saw by the change in the woman's face, that it had not failed. Evidently, she was one of those "undesirable aliens" who go in fear of a deportation order. He went on without pausing for her reply: "Well, you'd better get that straight, just as quick as you can. But I'm not concerned about your affairs now. All I want you to tell me is what time Emmoll called here on the night he was murdered, and what happened after that."

The woman looked far more frightened than before. "Murdered?" she echoed vaguely. "Emmoll? You mean the Jordans murder? He wasn't ever here in his life that I ever heard, and that's the truth as I'd take any oath that—"

"Never mind that. Just try to think. The Friday before last. Ever seen this man before?"

He produced a photograph of the murdered man, which the woman clearly recognized.

"Yes," she said, "that's Mr. Wilkinson. You don't mean—"

"I mean that's Emmoll. He may have called himself Wilkinson when he came here. I asked you what time he came on the night he got killed."

She appeared to think a moment, and answered straightly enough: "It must have been about ten, or perhaps a bit later than that. I was having supper when I came up to let him in."

"It was half-past ten. When did he go?"

"I'm sorry, sir, but I don't know that. Really, I don't. I have to come up to let people in when they haven't keys, but they let themselves out. I've no idea when he left. If it was much after eleven, I should be gone to bed, and I shouldn't hear."

That sounded likely enough, the inspector reasoned. And he had got the first point he required—the admission that Emmoll had been there, which the woman upstairs had denied when he had questioned her before. He felt that slowly, steadily, he moved on, step by step, to his goal.

"Very well," he said, "I'm going up now. I can find my own way."

On reaching the first floor he approached a door which bore the name MISS M. LE NOIR on a small brass plate, and tapped sharply. Almost as he did so, his hand tried the knob, and, the door being unlocked, he entered without further ceremony.

The woman whose eyes met his as he entered the room was slatternly, as was the untidy, overfurnished room. From too much drink and food, and too little exercise, her figure was becoming slackly obese; her chin sagged. Her attractions, for those who could overlook the rest, were her bronze-gold hair, which, unlike her complexion, was of authentic colour, and her large brown, spaniel-like eyes.

Inspector Combridge looked at her with a dislike he had no care to conceal. "Now, Miss Black," he said, "perhaps you'll tell me why you said Emmoll didn't come here last Friday week."

The woman, who had been writing a letter, drew the blotting paper across it, as she replied in an obstinate but wavering voice: "I said he hadn't because he hadn't, and you won't bully me into saying anything else."

"Nor Mr. Wilkinson?"

"It's nothing to do with me if he calls himself that. I suppose a gentleman can call himself what he likes."

"And they usually call themselves something else when they come here?"

She made no answer to that, and after a tense pause he added: "Then if that's all you've got to say, I shall have to ask you to come with me."

"You can't do that!" She had risen now, and her shrill, frightened voice was near to a scream. "You can't do that, when I've done nothing at all! It's not my fault if he came here when he did."

"It's your fault if you tell lies to the police and try to hide what happened."

"I'm not trying to hide anything. I don't know what happened. I tell you it isn't true!"

"You told me he hadn't been here at all."

"And what if I did? No one wants to be mixed up in a thing like that. There wasn't anything happened here."

Inspector Combridge drew a chair to the other side of the table from which the woman had risen. He sat down and motioned to her to do the same.

"Now look here, Miss Black," he said seriously, but in a less threatening voice than before, "I don't want to take you to Scotland Yard, and I certainly don't want to charge you, if you're an innocent woman, as I'm not doubting that you are. If you spend the night there it will be your own fault, unless it's because you've really done something wrong. But you've got to understand what the position is.

"A man comes to you, late at night—we know that for a fact—and next thing he's dead. You'll say he was dead a good way from here, but we know one thing for sure. He wasn't killed where he was found. And when we come to you for what help you can give, you put us to a lot of needless trouble by saying that he hadn't been here at all.

"Now if that isn't being an accomplice before or after the fact, it's a bit too near to be pleasant for you; and if you persist in saying he wasn't here, it may be considered to justify us in detaining you while we make further investigations, on suspicion of having been concerned in the crime."

The woman looked scared, but still irresolute, as though she might yet resolve that the dangers of silence were less than those of speech, but in the end she asked sullenly: "What do you want me to say?"

"I want you to tell the truth. Perhaps I'd better ask a few questions. What time did he come?"

"I don't remember exactly. It might have been near eleven, or not much after ten."

"Very well. About how long did he stay?"

"About three or four hours."

"Until two or half-past?"

"It might have been that."

"Rather a long time, was it not? Rather late to leave?"

"He said he was going to Southampton by car. He didn't want to start before then."

"Do you know who was going with him?"

"I don't know that anyone was. There'd be the driver, of course."

"He didn't mention who was driving him?"

"No. He didn't say anything about that. He was going by taxi, I suppose."

"Was anyone with him when he left the house?"

"Not that I know of. I don't think so. It wasn't likely there was. He just let himself out in the usual way."

"And while he was here? Who else did you have here at the time?"

"No one at all."

"You're quite certain of that?"

"Yes. Quite. He wouldn't have stayed if there'd been anyone else here."

"He gave you some money before he left?"

The woman looked sullen again, but answered reluctantly: "He only gave me five pounds."

"I didn't ask how much it was. That doesn't matter to me. It was English money, of course?"

"Yes. It was pound notes."

"Did he take them out of his pocket loose, or out of a wallet?"

"Out of his pocket book."

"Did you see whether there was other money there?"

"Yes. I saw there was a lot of American money. He didn't try to hide it at all."

"And that's all you can tell me?"

"Yes. I don't see what more I can. We just talked, and had supper, and then he went."

"You mean he had a meal here?"

"Yes. He always did when he came. There was nothing strange about that."

"I didn't suggest that there was anything strange, but it is a very important point, and in your favour rather than not. Now there's one more thing I want you to do. I want you to make me a list of all the men who've been here during the last two months, and whom—perhaps quite accidentally, and even without your knowledge—Emmoll may have met."

"I don't think I can do that."

"I'm afraid you must. But if they're innocent men it isn't likely that either you or they will hear anything more about it. I suppose there isn't one among them who makes up silly verses, especially when he's had too much to drink?"

"I wouldn't say that there's not."

"Well, I'll have him with the rest, and you must let me know which it is."

The list, with sufficient detail of descriptions attached to names of doubtful authenticity, took some time to extract from the woman's reluctant lips. When the inspector put it in his pocket at last, and rose to go, he was not sure whether he had obtained anything of value, or simply material on which a number of useful officers would be required to waste their time in the coming days. But, even so, he could not feel that the evening bad been uselessly spent. He had established beyond doubt where Emmoll had spent the earlier hours of the night, and, if it were true that he had consumed another meal there some hours after the dinner at the Savoy, it put forward the time of the murder to 5:00 or even 5:30 A.M.

He was yet far from sight of an arrest—far even from a guess of who the murderer could be—but he had still Miss Manly to question.

# CHAPTER VI.

THE home of Miss Prudence Manly was simple rather than luxurious in the details of its ordered regime, but it had the atmosphere of quiet sufficiency which settles upon the abodes of those to whom financial stringency is a remote condition far beyond the horizon of their own experience.

Miss Manly heard the inspector's name with a calmness of demeanour that showed no sign either of surprise or perturbation. She said, with a glance at the table on which lunch was already laid: "You'd better ask him in here, Ruth...and then lay another place."

Inspector Combridge, entering the room, encountered a tall spinster of middle age, with very blue eyes in a shrewd face.

"I have been," Miss Manly began, "in some doubt as to whether I should inform you of a discovery which I made last Friday. On reflection, I have decided that it is right to do so, and I should have rung you up after lunch, if you had not called."

"If it's anything to do with the Emmoll murder, I shouldn't think there could be much doubt about that," the inspector replied, in a tone which maintained the courtesy due to his hostess with some difficulty, as it strove with the indignation which such a remark must rouse in any normal official mind.

"Had it related to the murder alone," Miss Manly replied, with a smile that declined to resent the feeling she had aroused, "there wouldn't have been any doubt at all, though my decision would probably have been opposite to that which you would approve. The point was that it is a matter which—unless it be an absolute hoax, on which your opinion will be more valuable than mine—may be important to others who are innocent of any possible complicity with it. But I'd better tell you what it is, or you'll be expecting about ten times more than you're going to get."

Inspector Combridge's tense face showed new interest. "I should be obliged if you will," he said.

"There is a little wood at the foot of my garden—it is all within my property—and a footpath runs through it to the road. I don't mean the road you came on. It's another at right angles to it.

"The path is a short cut to the Meeting-House, or to Jordans. I sometimes use it myself, and so do the servants, but on the average it mayn't be used more than once a week, at this time of year, when it's rather bad walking. There's a key to the gate that opens to the road, but it's not often locked.

"People seldom attempt to enter the wood from the road, especially at this season, and the gate's usually left secured by nothing more than a latch.

"It was like that last Thursday, when I went through the wood because I was short of time.

"Someone, quite recently, or I should have had it destroyed before now, had thrown an old umbrella over from the road, unless it had blown over the fence, which I don't think it would. Anyhow, it had been lying among the bracken, not far from the path, and I had seen it there, and meant to tell the gardener to dear it away.

"On Thursday it was lying across the path. It had been wide open, not in very bad condition, but the handle had been broken away from the stick. Now it stood like a big mushroom, raised a few inches from the ground. I had a walking stick in my hand, and I tried to push the umbrella out of the way, but it seemed stuck.

"I bent down, and put a hand to it to pull it way, and found that the broken stick had been driven into the ground. When I pulled it out and turned the umbrella over into the bracken, I found that a piece of paper had been put on the path under it, held down by two stones, and with some writing on it in a rather large hand.

"I am long-sighted, and I could read what was written without disturbing it, or stooping closely—indeed, I could read it more easily than if I had been closer to it—and when I saw what it was I put the umbrella back, and locked the gate as I went out."

"So it's all still there?"

"It was there ten minutes before you called."

"Can you tell me what the writing says?"

"Not word for word. But it is a kind of confession, signed in the name of Tucker Emmoll, about a marriage that he seems to have denied previously. It also suggests that he was on the point of committing suicide when he wrote it."

"He didn't do that."

"Which makes it more likely, it seems to me, that the paper is a silly forgery."

"Yes. It certainly does. But I must say, Miss Manly, that you should have let us know this at once."

"I am inclined to think you are right. But unfortunately, I was not instantly sure, and I was taught from childhood not to act precipitately when in doubt of the right course of action to follow. And I don't suppose the delay will make any vital difference, even if I am not wasting your time with a silly hoax, which I can see you are inclined to expect it to be."

The rain had ceased, and a pale effort of winter sunshine was diffuse in a clouded sky, as Miss Manly rose to lead the way to the discovery she had made. As she did so, she turned to Inspector Combridge, to ask with some abruptness of manner: "By the way, I have told you that you saved me trouble by calling, but you haven't told me why you appeared so opportunely."

"We have many sources of information," the inspector answered with the vagueness which the position required.

"No doubt you have. What I am interested to know is why you thought I should be one."

"There cannot be many people in Jordans we haven't questioned more or less during the last ten days. I should have called on you before, I can assure you, if I had not heard that you were away over the weekend."

Miss Manly shook her head, unconvinced. "You mean," she said, "that if servants talk, it's no reason why you should follow their example. Well, Ruth's a good girl on the whole. Perhaps it's better that I shouldn't know. But if it had got about, it might have led to people coming into the wood."

The inspector restrained himself from the obvious reply that it showed how wrong she had been to delay informing the police of what she had found. He surmised correctly that the confidence which Miss Manly's maid had given to her friend Ethel, and which had come from her to Mr. Jellipot's ears, had been of too vague a nature, even if it had been more widely distributed, to lead to invasion of the little wood. He followed Miss Manly through the door, and down the length of a very orderly garden. They entered a little woodland path that wound through the boles of beeches now in winter nakedness, and too closely grown for their natural development, so that they became slender and tall as they reached upward to find the light.

Inspector Combridge saw nothing of them. They might have been in full leaf for all he knew. His eyes were on the path, seeking an old umbrella to which they came almost at once, still spreading itself mushroom-like with its outstretched ribs a few inches above the earth; for Miss Manly, thinking of the preservation of the document below, had planted the broken stick even more firmly than before. Carefully, Inspector Combridge lifted the umbrella aside, disclosing the document spread open upon the ground, held down by two stones of sufficient size, and showing little sign of weather damage. Raising it in a gloved hand, he read:

> *The worst deed of my life was that I denied that I had married Lucille Higgins. Now that I am about to end it, I admit that I married her on January $2^{nd}$, 1909, at Silver Springs, S.C., and that her son Edward Tucker Emmoll is my legitimate child.*
>
> *Tucker Emmoll*

Inspector Combridge read this singular document, which was undated and unaddressed, and, remembering how the clothes had been similarly deposited, congratulated himself upon the discretion that had withheld that incident from public knowledge, so that the idea of an imitative hoax could be eliminated. He had decided that the document was genuine, even before he turned it over and discovered that it had been written on the back of the receipted hotel bill which Emmoll must have settled immediately before he left.

He turned to Miss Manly to say: "Yes, I've no doubt that this is genuine. I'm much obliged to you for reporting it. I don't suppose there'll be any need to say anything about the short delay that has occurred, especially if you'll do me the favour of not mentioning it to anyone."

"Yes, you can trust me for that. You couldn't do me a greater favour than by taking it away, so that I should not hear of it again."

"I don't know that you need hear of it again, unless circumstances should arise which would require you to give evidence of where it was found. But I would like to search a bit further round here, and to be sure that I shall be undisturbed. Could you open the gate at the end of this path for me, and send my car round into the other road when it arrives? I should be grateful if you'd tell the man, rather than give a message to the mud."

Miss Manly said she would open the gate herself, which she went on to do. She agreed as readily to send the car round into the other road. Beyond that, when she returned to the house, she gave such tasks to her household staff, as insured that the inspector would be undisturbed.

After that, she put the whole matter from her mind. It had become Inspector Combridge's problem, not hers—and a sufficiently difficult one he found it to be.

# CHAPTER VII.

IT WAS late in the evening when Chief Detective-Inspector Combridge returned to London, and made his way to Scotland Yard. He knew Superintendent Davis, with whom he had already been on the telephone to report his latest discovery, would be waiting to see him. But as he reviewed the latest development he did not feel himself to be a Chief Detective-Inspector. He felt only that he was a maddeningly baffled, bewildered man.

A thorough search of the little wood had disclosed no evidence that it had been the scene of Tucker Emmoll's death; nor had it supplied any clue either to the tragedy itself or to the deposit of the document, unless in the impression of a man's shoe at the side of the narrow path. This was at a place where a patch of liquid mud had caused its wearer to step aside, and the footprint, being partly over-shadowed by a branch of low-growing yew, had remained undamaged by subsequent rain. It was a clear impression of a lightly-made shoe of medium size. A time might come when it would be evidence of a damning weight. But, at present, it was of no assistance at all. To compare it with the shoes of some millions of Englishmen, any one of whom might possibly have been in that little wood during the past week, was beyond even the imagination of Inspector Combridge's patient persistence.

Still, a time might come! Certainly, evidences continued to accumulate, which had the one satisfactory consequence that he could not be judged to be making no progress in the investigation. The trouble was that they appeared to lead nowhere. Indeed, they rather suggested further confusion than elucidation of the problem he had to solve.

The document that had now been found was almost certainly genuine—he would know definitely when it had been compared with authentic specimens of the dead man's handwriting, and when he had inquired concerning the existence of Lucille Higgins—but, if so, what was to be made of the suggestion that Tucker Emmoll had been about to end his own life? It was so utterly discordant with the other facts, such as the position in which the body had been found. And, if he had done so, how and with whom could he have arranged to place his clothes and this confession as they had been subsequently discovered?

Inspector Combridge's usual difficulty in such investigations had been that theories were easy to form, but facts were harder to find. Here he had facts, even to excess, but a single plausible theory was beyond his ingenuity to set up. He was confronted by an obvious murder. An identified victim. A plethora of dramatic fact. And he had no theory, and no suspect!

It was with this chastening realization that he entered the superintendent's room, and encountered an atmosphere of congratulatory approval which he had not anticipated. Superintendent Davis, a massive man, very keen of wit, but with a delusive slowness of speech and movement, was not easily stirred to excesses of optimism or depression. He had seen too many difficult cases solved, either by luck or skill; too many, that had looked simple at first, pass on to the quickly forgotten category of unsolved crimes. Now he saw evidence accumulate in a way which, to his experienced mind, was indication of final triumph. He had learned not to despond while any line of inquiry was incomplete. And here was Combridge not only with a further dramatic discovery, but such a one as pointed to new people and unsuspected facts—a new line of investigation which might lead straight to the criminal.

"I don't know how you got on the track of these," he said, as the inspector laid the hotel bill with its curious endorsement upon his desk alongside the old umbrella, "but you seem to be getting towards the solution of what's likely to rank as the most sensational murder of modern times. The public may think we're a bit slow, but they'll forget that when we pull all the tricks out of the hat. But before we talk about these, you'll like to know that we've got some more information about that fellow George Tipper that's rather interesting, though I'm not going so far as to suppose he had anything to do with the case.

"You know that his last employer in London gave him a fairly good character—the sort that doesn't mean much either way. And the man he was with before was laid up with influenza, so it was only this morning that Richards was able to get to see him.

"He found him quite willing to tell us all he knew, and, as far as his own opinion went, he wasn't at all sure that Tipper's a bad sort. But he says that while he was with him he was prosecuted for cruelty to a dog. Though the case was dismissed through the evidence not being quite conclusive, he was unpopular in consequence. After he'd made an assault upon one of his fellow-employees in consequence of something he heard said—he gave him a smashing blow on the face that broke his nose—the atmosphere was such that he was told he'd better leave, which he did.

"But, apart from that, there was nothing against him, except that he was apt to get drunk at the weekends. I understand he's a very capable man at superintending the decease of a pig and disjointing it subsequently, and he doesn't quarrel when he's sober and left to himself."

"It doesn't really amount to much, unless he makes verses when he gets drunk."

"It doesn't amount to anything."

"There's the fact that he could have been out during the night without anyone seeing him go or return."

"Which is no evidence that he did. The fact is that we shouldn't have given him two thoughts if we hadn't been up against a blank wall as to what really did happen."

Inspector Combridge did not dispute this, but it caused his mind to revert to the mood in which he had entered the room. He said: "And as far as I can see we're still at the same spot."

"You're never at a blank wall while you've got a line of inquiry that's not followed up. We've got to find out what this confession means, and by the time we've done that we may have let in some daylight on other things."

\* \* \* \* \* \* \*

The event proved the soundness of Superintendent Davis' experienced prophecy. A long cable to the New York police was followed by two days during which no progress was made, beyond comparing the newly discovered document with authentic specimens of Tucker Emmoll's writing and arriving at a decided opinion that, although it was less firm in character—which was not surprising in view of the circumstances under which it purported to have been written—there was no reasonable doubt that it was in the hand of the dead man. And this received strong confirmation when a cable arrived from New York:

> LUCILLE HIGGINS BROUGHT SUIT AGAINST EMMOLL THREE YEARS AGO TO ESTABLISH MARRIAGE WITH HIM AND PATERNITY OF HER CHILD EDWARD STOP SUIT WAS DISMISSED FOR LACK OF EVIDENCE AFTER EMMOLL HAD DENIED MARRIAGE ON OATH STOP LUCILLE RECENTLY PROSECUTED FOR PERSISTING IN USE OF EMMOLL'S NAME AND SENTENCED FOURTEEN DAYS DETENTION AFTER REFUSAL TO PAY FINE IMPOSED STOP EDWARD HIGGINS THREATENED REVENGE ON EMMOLL AND WAS ROUGHLY HANDLED BY EMMOLL'S BODYGUARD ON ATTEMPTING TO FORCE INTERVIEW STOP MADE SECOND ATTEMPT AND FOUND EMMOLL HAD LEFT FOR EUROPE STOP FURTHER CABLE FOLLOWS.

It was only a few hours after the receipt of this cable, and just as Combridge, who had been out when it arrived, was discussing it with Superintendent Davis, that a second one arrived from the same source:

EDWARD HIGGINS SAILED FOR LONDON ON AMERICAN BANKER TENTH DECEMBER LAST STOP LANDED TWENTIETH STOP IS LOOKED TO RETURN ON AMERICAN MERCHANT FEBRUARY SEVENTH.

"Which," Superintendent Davis remarked, "is today."

"The boats of the American Merchant line leave King George V dock," Inspector Combridge added, "every Friday about midnight, I believe, varying somewhat according to the run of the tide." He glanced at a round clock on the wall as he concluded. "So we've just got time."

"Time for what?"

"Time to ask him—Edward Higgins, or Emmoll—a few questions.

"Yes. You can do that. Getting him to answer them is another matter. What will you do to prevent him sailing, if he has sense enough to refuse?"

"He won't refuse. Not unless he can't answer without leading himself straight to the noose. He'll be too inclined to think of how they'd handle him in his own land. Third degree, and all that."

"That's likely enough."

"Besides, if he does sail, we shall know where he's to be found for the next week, and a bit more—they're ten-day boats."

"Or, if they call at Boston, a day less before he could land."

"Yes. We must watch that."

"You'll have to remember too that he's an American citizen, and they are American boats. He's out of our hands as soon as the three-mile limit is passed, if not before that, and you won't get him back without a lot more reason than we've got now."

"We may have that, when we've made a few inquiries about his movements during the last fortnight. But he hasn't sailed yet," the inspector answered, as he reached for the telephone, and called the Passenger Office of the United States Lines. He felt that he was on the right track at last.

Not that he had wasted his time till now. All the miscellaneous facts so patiently and laboriously accumulated would fall, one by one, into place, and would become meshes of the net by which the criminal would be caught.

Superintendent Davis heard him on the telephone two minutes later: "Yes. Edward Tucker Higgins. That's the name. Yes. So I understood of course you have his London address? Yes. Willing's Hotel. Bloomsbury Street. Yes, I've got that. No, not unless you hear further from us, as it's quite likely you will."

He put down the receiver, saying: "They don't sail till eleven-thirty. Passengers can go on board this afternoon, if they like, but they seldom go much before nine. Higgins is intending to sail. He called in yesterday to select his cabin. It's more likely than not that I shall find him at his hotel now. I've got the address. If I do, I'll bring him along and we'll question him where we've got some witnesses. It seems that he isn't as obstinate as his mother. He calls himself Higgins, not Emmoll. But that might be because he couldn't get a passport, except in his mother's name."

He ended with the realization that the superintendent's attention was not given to him, but concentrated upon a cable that had been brought in during the telephone conversation.

The superintendent gazed at it, rubbing his chin. He said: "Here's a bit more about your young friend Higgins. They're certainly hustling in New York. I suppose they're alive to the fact that he means to say good-bye to us tonight."

Inspector Combridge asked: "What is it? Is it any use?" with more impatience than was quite seemly in addressing his superior officer. But he was both curious to know what it was, and in some haste to get through to Willing's Hotel, to learn whether Mr. Higgins were still to be found there.

Not answering him directly, the superintendent said, with what appeared to be a maddening irrelevance: "You told me how Miss Prudence Manly impressed you. I wish you'd say it again."

Inspector Combridge stared, hesitated, and had the wit to see that there must be more reason in the request than he was able to understand. He answered with a controlled impatience: "I should describe her as a well-educated Quaker lady, in comfortable circumstances, with rather more conscience than most people would find exactly comfortable to carry about, but not a bad sort all the same."

"Age?"

"Anything between forty and fifty. I couldn't say more nearly than that. She's not the sort who tries to look young."

"You didn't think her a fool?"

"No. Quite the other way."

"And a woman of good character? I mean of integrity. One who wouldn't try to plant anything on you, or lead you a dance?"

"Yes. I should say there's no question of that."

"She didn't happen to mention that she'd ever been in the States?"

"No. The question didn't come up at all."

"Nor known anything of the Emmoll family, father or son?"

"No, she certainly didn't."

"Well, that's how I understood you before. It's some satisfaction to know that I'm not going deaf. And I used to think you could sum a woman up as well as most of us can!"

Superintendent Davis picked up the cablegram as he said this, and passed it across the desk. Inspector Combridge read:

LUCILLE HIGGINS STATES THAT HER SON IS VISITING LONDON ON BUSINESS REPRESENTING THE TEMPLAR ENGINEERING COMPANY SOMERTON MICHIGAN STOP ALSO TO SEE MISS PRUDENCE MANLY WHOM HE MET HERE LAST YEAR AND IS ENGAGED TO MARRY STOP LUCILLE IS CONFIDENT THAT HER SON DID NOT INTEND TO MEET TUCKER

EMMOLL AND HAD NO CONNECTION WITH
THE MURDER THIS FOR YOUR INFORMATION
WITHOUT OPINION FROM US STOP WE ARE
MAKING FURTHER INQUIRIES.

"I assume," the superintendent asked presently, "that your opinion of Miss Manly is somewhat changed?"

"No," Inspector Combridge answered, with unusual obstinacy, "I don't know that it is."

"You see that the confession which she found in the wood is likely, if its genuineness can be sustained, to confer a fortune upon the much younger man whom she intends to marry?"

"Yes, that's evident."

"And you still think it was dumped in her wood by a mere chance, as she led you to believe?"

The inspector did not answer directly. He said: "I think it's the craziest case I was ever on." He added, as Superintendent Davis regarded him with a faintly humorous smile: "But that's no reason why I shouldn't get hold of Edward Higgins as soon as I can."

"No. I should say it's an additional reason why you should."

He thought, "And it mightn't be a bad idea to have the lady here too."

But he did not mention this, because his opinion of Miss Manly had become radically different from that which the inspector had expressed and seemed so unwilling to yield. He thought he had better handle this in his own way.

# CHAPTER VIII.

INSPECTOR COMBRIDGE: had a few words on the telephone with P. G. Willing, hotel proprietor, and learned that Edward Higgins was in the writing room, evidently occupied in final correspondence before leaving England; and that he had just asked for tea to be brought to him there in half an hour's time.

The victim appeared to be unsuspicious, but the inspector had learned to trust no man more than was unavoidable. Though he received a rather nervously emphatic assurance from Willing that his inquiry would not be communicated to the gentleman whom it concerned, he took the precaution of implying that it might be an hour or more before he would arrive. "Don't hurry that tea, Mr. Willing. Make it a bit more than the half-hour rather than less," he said, and lost no time in entering the fastest car that was available at New Scotland Yard, reckoning that some minutes should be enough to cover the distance to Bloomsbury Street.

Superintendent Davis sat silent for a brief minute after he had gone, reviewing the singular development indicated by the discovery in Miss Manly's grounds, and the three cables upon his desk.

He appreciated the action of his New York colleagues in acquainting him so promptly with the ostensible reasons for Edward Higgins'—or Emmoll's—visit to England. Doubtless they had thought both to apprise him of the possibility of the young man's innocence, and to give information by which to check the veracity of whatever explanations he might offer. But the superintendent saw that the potential significance of the final cable was radically altered by the document to which Miss Manly had led the way, and by the place and circumstances in which it was said to have been found.

Having considered these facts, which were of a separate innocence, but became sinister in combination, he proceeded to act with his usual promptness. He reached for the telephone and asked the operator to ring up Miss Prudence Manly.

A moment later he heard an unexcited, pleasantly modulated voice say: "Yes. Miss Manly speaking. Is that Chief Inspector Combridge?"

"No. This is Superintendent Davis. I have Inspector Combridge's report of the document, which you were good enough to bring to his notice, before me now. I should be glad to have an opportunity of talking it over with you before we do anything further. Could you come up to town this afternoon? I believe there are plenty of trains from Seer Green, but perhaps you'd prefer to come by your own car, or I could arrange for one to be sent from Beaconsfield that would bring you in."

"I'm afraid it wouldn't be convenient this afternoon. As a matter of fact, I have a social engagement this evening. But I could give you a call tomorrow or—no, that's Saturday—on Monday afternoon, if that's convenient to you."

"I'm afraid, Miss Manly, I must ask you to put the social engagement aside. I think you'll see that this is the more important matter."

"Yes. I suppose it is. But actually I don't see that I can do anything further to help you if I come. I gave the inspector all the information I could at the time. And—pardon me, I don't mean to be rude—but if it's so important to see me at once, don't you think you could come to me?"

"No, Miss Manly, I don't. I don't want to be rude, either, but there may be someone here this afternoon whom I should like you to meet, and, in a matter of this importance, I think I must ask you to put other engagements aside."

There was a moment's pause, and then, in a voice changed only by a slight note of annoyance which could not be considered unnatural under the most innocent presumption, Miss Manly replied:

"Well, if I can really be of any important assistance to you, I won't refuse. I can get to Marylebone at five-ten. You want me to come to Scotland Yard? No, I can't say I do; but I expect any policeman will tell me the way there!" There was a sound of light laughter, pleasant and unperturbed. "And I'm to ask for Superintendent Davis? Yes, I'll remember that."

Superintendent Davis left the telephone, with a feeling of satisfaction in having persuaded her to come, and a clearer understanding of his subordinate's report. Certainly the voice was consistent with the description which he had received. And there had been no sound of nervousness, even after the hint that he had given of the unnamed individual she was to meet. And incidentally it appeared evident that she had not been seeing her lover off on the boat. Or was that the "social engagement" she had been unwilling to put aside? Superintendent Davis, without any reason that he could formulate to his own satisfaction, was inclined to think not. But he thought again that when it should go into court, as he had no doubt that it was soon destined to do, it would be the most sensational trial of recent years.

As it now stood, Combridge had hit the nail on the head squarely enough when he had described it as the craziest case he had ever known. But that aspect would be reduced as, one by one, the remaining facts were discovered and fell into place. In the end, there would be no more than an experienced counsel could make plausible and clear to a normal jury, perhaps with illustrations of previous crimes of ferocity, or insanity. He could imagine Denis Hartlin doing it with cold, dispassionate, analytical skill. He thought that a good deal that was puzzling now would be clear before he should go home tonight. He began to write down a series of questions to which one or the other of his expected visitors might find it difficult to give convincing answers—especially Miss Manly. He saw that if Edward Higgins did not convict himself by his own admissions, it might not be easy to make much progress with him. But Miss Manly was in a different position. *"Do you tell me seriously, Miss Manly—"* he wrote. *"Do you really ask me to believe—?"*

Yes, her replies should be very interesting to hear.

Thinking with some complaisance that, whatever might be said against his profession, it must be admitted that it was not dull, Superintendent Davis rang for his tea.

\* \* \* \* \* \* \*

P. G. Willing, a plump, small-eyed man, known inevitably as Piggie Willing to his acquaintances, met Inspector Combridge at the reception desk with the assurance that Mr. Higgins was still in the writing room. His manner was such as to remind the inspector that Edward Higgins was not yet a convicted criminal. Combridge said rather sharply:

"Well, I've not come to arrest him, you know. I only want a few words with him, and wished to make sure that he would not have gone out when I called. How long has he been staying here?"

Now that he was sure there could be no escape, he felt in no haste to confront the probable son and almost equally probable murderer of Tucker Emmoll. He would proceed in his usual orderly manner, learning all he could of the man he was about to meet.

"He came just before Christmas."

The register lay at the hotel manager's hand, and was promptly opened and passed over the counter for Inspector Combridge's observation. He read the entry: "Edward Tucker Higgins, U.S.A. citizen," and a Brooklyn address, with less attention to the words themselves than to the handwriting in which they were entered.

As he did so, he put one interesting query out of his mind. Had the document which had been so curiously planted in Miss Manly's wood been forged by the son of the murdered man to establish his own inheritance? It was a plausible idea, now that he knew of Edward Higgins' engagement. And he had known cases in which the handwriting of parent and child had shown close resemblances. This might be least likely when they had lived apart and educated in different ways, but the possibility remained. He saw that one of the strongest reasons which had led him to regard it as a genuine confession had been the resemblance between the way it, and the clothes, had been deposited. But if the murder had been committed by Edward Higgins, and the parcel of clothes left by him on the hill-side path, might he not have forged the confession, and then put it where it would be found in similar manner? And did not this theory explain what had been the most puzzling feature of the document while it had been regarded as a genuine confession—the suggestion of self-destruction?

It was almost certain that Tucker Emmoll had not taken his own life, and, if not, why should he have expressed such an intention, or why should he have written in anticipation of death? But if the theory of forgery were admitted, what more natural than that the murderer should produce the idea of self-destruction, for his own protection if suspicion should subsequently approach him?

It was a theory that would explain much, and to which there was only one serious objection that Inspector Combridge observed and made no effort to minimize. He had no wish to persuade himself to a false conclusion. If Edward Higgins had forged that document with the intention of securing the fortune which, in all probability, was justly his, and from which he was only barred by a mistaken legal decision—a fortune the acquisition of which might have been as powerful a motive in urging him to the crime as the desire to avenge his mother's wrongs—would he have deposited the paper in his fiancée's grounds?

It seemed improbable, and yet it became less so on a closer examination. In the first place, it was of vital importance that the document should be found by someone who would report it to the police. Planted on a stranger's grounds, it might have fallen into hands which would not recognize its importance. It might be found, as the parcel of clothes had been, by children, who might destroy it or throw it aside. It might have been trodden down unregarded, or become sodden with rain or melting snow.

No If Edward Higgins depended upon that advice for securing the fortune he was determined to have, he would wish to make very sure that the document would be found in the right way.

Besides that, would the risk appear to him to be as great as in fact it was? He had no cause to think that suspicion of the murder would fall on himself, no reason to suppose that the police had any knowledge of his acquaintance with Prudence Manly. And, in fact, they would have had none but for the activities of the New York police, of which he could have no knowledge at all!

The patient ingenuity of Inspector Combridge's mind developed a further theory, which became plausible enough when he remembered that he was dealing with no ordinary criminal. Suppose the idea was that, to the eyes of the public and the police, Edward Higgins had intended it to appear that he would meet Prudence Manly for the first time in consequence of this confession having been found by her? That it would appear that their acquaintance, ripening into romance, arose from that cause alone? Who would think to look behind the event, on the improbable assumption that they had been acquainted previously?

He was not entirely satisfied with the probability of this idea, but he knew that even the most ingenious murderers are apt to do improbably foolish things. And the fact, more stubborn than any theory, remained. It was in Miss Manly's grounds that the document—so carefully protected by the old umbrella—had been found.

It was with these thoughts that he had looked with more interest at the handwriting of Edward Higgins than at the words written in the hotel register. But he had to accept the fact that what he saw gave no support to the theories which he had been formulating.

The writing he saw was small, neat, regular, and yet of a pronounce character, very different from the ill-formed emphatic hand of the older man.

It proved nothing, either way. Edward Higgins might be a most skillful forger. He might have accomplices. Indeed, he *must* have had them. How could the murder and the subsequent stripping and exposure of the body have been the work of one man? He might—but there were so many "mights"! Let the theories wait. It was facts he was seeking now.

He passed the register back to Willing with the question: "I suppose he's been here regularly all the time from that date?"

"Yes. At least, he's kept on his room here. He's been away for a night or more sometimes. Went to Glasgow once, or at least that's what he said."

"Have you learned anything of what business he's been doing here?"

"Not much. He's not one to talk. He's pleasant enough, but the kind who keeps to himself. I believe he represents some American firm that manufactures machines, though I don't know what kind they are. I daresay you know more than I do about that."

"Templar Engineering Co.?"

"Yes, that's the name."

"Well, that's all right. I've no doubt they're a good firm. Has he had many visitors here?"

"No. Not many. Not to notice, that is."

"Any ladies?"

"No. We don't allow that sort of thing here."

"I didn't suggest anything disreputable. We know nothing wrong goes on here. I wish all hotels were run the same way. But you don't remember any lady calling to see him, or perhaps ringing him up?"

"No, I can't say I do. But it might not have come under my notice. I'll make inquiries if it's important. The porter or the telephone operator would be most likely to know."

"It mayn't matter. If it does, I'll ask you again. I suppose you'd have a record of any nights that he was away from the hotel?"

"Not necessarily. Not when a guest pays for his room. But I don't say there aren't ways we could find it out. We book the breakfasts, for one thing. Not by names, but by the numbers of the rooms, which comes to much the same."

"Well, you might let me have the dates when Mr. Higgins hasn't had breakfast here. And any occasions when he's come in during the night. I suppose you have a night porter?"

"No, we don't. Not a regular one. We keep open until twelve-thirty, and anyone coming in after that has to make special arrangements."

"You mean tip the porter to wait up for him?"

"Yes. That's about it."

"Well, find out all you can for me in a discreet way. I just want the truth. I shan't thank anyone for remembering something that didn't happen. Higgins is rather a heavy drinker, isn't he?"

Piggie Willing stared at the question in evident surprise. "I didn't think," he said, "that he drank at all. I wouldn't call him that kind."

Inspector Combridge concealed a natural disappointment at this reply. He said easily: "Oh, but most of us do, more or less. I suppose you'll think it's a sillier question still if I ask whether he makes up rhymes?"

"I wouldn't say but he does. You could ask Bessie—that's the chambermaid—about that."

"You mean he makes up verses for her?"

"No. I didn't mean that." He added, with some hesitation: "If a man throws anything into the wastepaper basket, I don't see that he can complain."

"You mean if it's read by those who empty it?"

"Yes. It's what they're likely to do."

"Yes. I expect it is. I may have a word with Bessie before long. But please don't say anything to her till I do. I think I'll see Mr. Higgins now, and I'll trust you to keep this conversation confidential."

With these words Inspector Combridge passed into the writing-room, leaving Piggie Willing highly excited and very curious as to what manner of crime had drawn the attention of the law to his American guest. Willing was a little doubtful whether it had been wise to remember that Bessie sometimes giggled over the rhyming attempts which she fished out of the wastepaper basket of number forty, for the amusement of herself and her fellow-servants. How would it sound if it should come out in court that he allowed such spying upon his guests?

# CHAPTER IX.

INSPECTOR COMBRIDGE entered the writing-room, which was vacant except for one man who did not look up, but said irritably: "I've ordered some tea twice already. I thought you'd know what I meant when I rang again, without coming to ask."

"I'm not the waiter," Inspector Combridge replied, and a young man looked up and said apologetically, with a perceptible American accent:

"Oh, I beg your pardon. The fact is that I've rung three times for some tea, and I'm wanting to get out in a few minutes. The service is so good here as a rule that it makes it seem more annoying when it goes lame on its legs."

At that moment the waiter entered and Mr. Higgins turned his attention to him, receiving a somewhat unconvincing apology with: "Well, don't waste any more time. Bring it along now, or I shan't have it at all."

Inspector Combridge observed a young man of slim, athletic build, but with the face of one who worked at a desk rather than in open air. Looking at him with the puzzled curiosity which he would often feel at the first sight of a criminal whom it was his duty to run to earth, he could see little to identify him with the perpetrator of that grotesquely indecent murder, or the ribald rhyme. Years ago, he would have said to himself that it was incredible that such a man should be concerned in so foul a crime. But he had learned since then how little in appearance and manner separates the murderer from his fellowmen, particularly so when he can be observed—as he

observed Edward Higgins now—without knowledge that he is suspected, or being in any fear of arrest.

He knew that if this man should be convicted of his father's
murder, there would be pictures of him in the newspapers, representing him as of a bestial depravity. It would all be done with a few
skillful lines from the artist's pencil, while the portrait would still be
there. It was what the public expected to have. It was hard on the
relatives of a convicted man. Perhaps hard on the man himself. But
would it be really false? Might not the artist see that which was truly
there, though it was hidden from other eyes? All he could see in the
face of Edward Higgins was a squareness of chin which could be
made to look brutal with little change, and a hint of moroseness
about the mouth. It was no more than the look of one who might
take life hardly, who might make it hard for himself; who might not
be easily compliant to the tempers or inclinations of those around
him. To one who had no reason to suspect him of such a crime it
would be no worse than that.

"I should like a few words with you, Mr. Higgins," he said. "I
suppose we shall be sufficiently private here?"

Higgins looked slightly irritated, slightly surprised. He said,
"Yes?" in a vague way. "As a matter of fact, I'm going out in a few
minutes. What is it you want to say?"

Inspector Combridge produced a card. "Perhaps you'll understand better if you know who I am."

Higgins glanced at it, and then for the first time really looked at
his visitor. He handed back the card—an action that the inspector
inwardly resented, as though treating him as one who could be put
aside with ease—and answered without emotion: "I understand who
you are. I don't understand what you want, if you mean that. But
there's no reason you shouldn't sit down. I see they're bringing me
the tea I've been ordering for the last hour. Perhaps while I have that
you can tell me what the trouble is?"

He had risen from the writing-desk as he spoke, and moved to a
lower chair beside which the waiter had now drawn a little table on
which he had deposited the tea-tray. Inspector Combridge waited till
they were alone once more before he answered, as he sat down in a

nearby chair: "I don't think you can really be ignorant of the only business which would be likely to bring me here."

"I certainly am. I'm not aware of having done anything, or left anything undone, which would be of interest to the British police. But if you're anxious for me to guess, I should say—no, I don't see why I should. If you've got any business with me, I suppose you can say what it is yourself without any guessing from me."

"It's about the Emmoll murder."

"Then I should have made the right guess. But I can't give you any help about that, and I see no reason why I should go out of my way to try."

"Then why did you think it was that matter which brought me here?"

"Because I'm sorry to say that I am that man's son. It's not a thing that I'm likely to boast of, and the American law has decided that it isn't true. While that decision stands, I don't see that you've any claim on me to interest myself in the matter, and I tell you plainly I don't intend to lift a finger to help you. I don't think I would if I knew who the murderer is. As a matter of fact, you've come a bit late. I'm going back to New York tonight."

"Perhaps that's for us to say."

Higgins was roused by that. His face flushed with anger. He said: "You mean you might hold me as a witness? But I know nothing. I couldn't help you in any way."

"I didn't suggest anything of the kind. We don't hold witnesses in this country. If you can satisfy us that you had nothing to do with Tucker Emmoll's death, we've no more to say."

"Why should you suppose I have?"

"I didn't come here to answer questions. I came here to ask you to come with me to Scotland Yard. We've a few questions to ask you, and when they're answered we shall know where we stand."

"Do you mean that I'm under arrest?"

"No. We don't arrest anyone in this country until we feel sure we've got the right man, especially if they're willing to give us a plain answer to whatever questions we think it necessary to ask."

"And if I refuse to come with you? What do you propose to do then?"

"If you are innocent it would be a very foolish attitude to adopt."

"Perhaps it would, but that isn't what I asked."

"If you decline to come with me, I must ask for your passport, and an assurance that you will not leave the country without our permission."

"And who would pay my hotel bill for the next week?"

"I don't suppose there'd be any difficulty about that."

"Oh, but there would! I'm off home because I've spent all the money I brought."

"I understand that you are here as the representative of one of the leading engineering firms in America."

"I represent the Templar Engineering Co. They don't pay my expenses. I came to do business for them at my own risk."

"You must have been very anxious to come."

"So I was."

"And has the business proved to be worth the journey?"

"Yes, it sure has."

"And may I ask if this business was your only reason for coming here at your own risk."

"You may ask anything you like."

"And you refuse to reply?"

"Not at all. Most Americans are glad to have a look at this country."

"Nothing beyond that?"

"And of seeing friends here."

While he asked these questions the inspector's mind had been debating what course he should take if Higgins should refuse to go with him. He did not find him unwilling to answer questions now, but he knew that Superintendent Davis was expecting that he would be brought into the intimidating precincts of Scotland Yard— perhaps to be confronted by the woman to whom he was engaged, and who might have given answers at variance from his own.

He did not wish to be the first to mention Miss Manly, nor did he wish, at this point, to allude to the confession so strangely found on her premises. Probably Higgins knew that Miss Manly had handed the document to the police. Probably he was debating, at the back of his mind, what connection there might be between that event and his present interrogation. But he could not know. He could not know whether the fact of his engagement, or of his previous acquaintance with Prudence Manly, was known to the English police. It was better that he should continue to doubt.

But if he were obstinate—here was the difficulty—if he would neither say anything to incriminate himself nor consent to be conducted to police headquarters, it would be a course of very doubtful legality to attempt to force him to go. For however strong the vague suspicion against him might be, Inspector Combridge realized that legally there was no case against him. Of course, the position might soon be radically changed; even in a few hours. The result of inquiries as to his night absences from the hotel, the verses that the chambermaid had retrieved from the wastepaper basket, possible admissions by Prudence Manly—many things might come to light now that they were on the right track, of which he had little doubt. But the fact remained that there was a deplorable paucity of legal evidence on which to arrest or detain him now; little on which the most complaisant magistrate could be asked to approve the arrest and to grant a remand.

Being in this difficulty, and recognizing that he had met a man who would not be easy either to coax or drive, and who, in all probability, knew that his chance of freedom—perhaps of life—depended upon his courage and coolness now, Inspector Combridge went on with a determination to induce Edward Higgins to enter his waiting car.

"I want you to understand," he said, "that we are not making any accusation against you. If we intend to make a criminal charge, it is our custom to give a warning that anything that is said to us may be brought in evidence when the case is heard. But all men are innocent by English law until their guilt can be proved. It is our custom, when suspicion first points in their direction, to invite them to

give any explanation they may desire, and to regard them as innocent men unless we know such explanation to be false, or until we
have tested it and found it to be so. But if a suspected person declines to answer our inquiries we are disposed to assume—and in
this we find we are rarely wrong—that he has been silent because he
would have incriminated himself had he spoken freely."

"Well, I have not refused to answer you. But I tell you again
that I have no knowledge of the crime."

"Still, I must ask you to listen for a moment while I—"

"Perhaps you'd like some tea while you talk?"

"No, thank you. I—"

"Well, you're the first I've met. I thought all Britishers were
alike in that. In fact, I've got to like the custom myself. I score it up
to the fog. Maybe you won't eat with a man when you've been set to
frame him? Now one of our cops—"

"We don't frame anyone, as you call it, here."

"No? It's how you use the word. I don't see how you can miss
doing it more or less at your game. And now let's hear the book of
words."

"We have information, Mr. Higgins, that your mother brought
an unsuccessful suit against Tucker Emmoll in which she alleged
that she was his wife, and that you are his legitimate son. After that,
he prosecuted her because she went on using his name, and she was
fined, and then imprisoned because she refused to pay.

"I don't know who was right or wrong, but you took your
mother's side, as it was quite natural you should, and—"

"You see I *did*."

"You mean you did know? Well, I'll not question that. As a
matter of fact, it makes the motive all the stronger. But if we've got
the tale right, you threatened to have revenge on your father—I
don't mind calling him that, if you say he was—after he'd put your
mother in jail. You tried to force an interview with him in such a
manner that you were thrown out, and rather roughly handled by the
bodyguard that I believe it is quite usual for men of his kind to keep
for their own protection."

"Well, you've got it right, so far. You haven't lost much time digging things up. I'll hand you that. And you'll understand why I didn't order a wreath. But it doesn't follow that I had anything to do with the way he died."

"No. We don't say it does. But when we have to add that you followed him here, after you'd failed to get near him in your own country—well, you can't wonder that we feel we should like to know more than we do now."

"And that's all you've got?"

"No. It's a long way from that. There are other things which seem difficult to explain, but we wish to give you every opportunity of doing so. We don't wish to judge any man before we've heard what he's got to say."

"Other things? Such as—?"

But this was the point at which Inspector Combridge wished to avoid reply. He knew that the element of surprise might be of decisive importance, and that it was a matter which Superintendent Davis—particularly if he had been successful in getting Miss Manly to come in—would wish to handle in his own way. Dealing a minor card from a thin hand, be said: "Well, there are certain absences from this hotel—absences during the night—"

He knew that "uncertain absences," the present state of his information, would have been the truer word, but he had found that these random shots would often disconcert the wiliest opponent.

Higgins, if he were disconcerted, concealed it well. "You mean that when I go to Glasgow, I'm not here? I don't see any crime in that. When I came over here there wasn't any bargain that I should be stopping at this hotel."

"Only to Glasgow?"

"I haven't said that, and that's what I mean by trying to frame something on me. Now see here, officer, if I'm making a right guess, you haven't got anything on me at all, and you're just trying to get a case out of my own mouth, and you're wasting time. I've had time to think now and, unless you arrest me for something I know that I haven't done, I'm not coming with you. You tell me you can't hold witnesses here. If that's so, it seems to me that you're asking me to arrest myself to save you getting the blame later."

Declining to react to the sound of rising temper in the emphasis of this protest—which, indeed, he rather welcomed, having had frequent occasion to observe that discretions lessen as passions rise— the inspector continued quietly: "And there are certain verses—"

For the first time, he felt that he had passed his opponent's guard. Higgins looked startled, flushed angrily, and faltered in his reply. "Verses?" he echoed. "I haven't the least idea what you mean. But I've finished tea now, and as far as I'm concerned there's no more to be said. I've given you all the time I can, and I've come to the conclusion that you've been trying a silly bluff."

He rose as he spoke, pushing back the little table with its empty tea-tray, but Inspector Combridge made no similar motion. He was not sure of the significance of what he heard. Had the mention of verses warned the man that the conversation was becoming too dangerous to continue, or was it no more than the natural shame or indignation of a man accused, either rightly or wrongly, of such a habit? He knew that he himself would resent an imputation of writing poetry more acutely than if he were charged with petty larceny or the forging of checks.

Leaving a subject which it was clear that Higgins would not discuss, he said: "If you persist in this attitude, you have to consider not only your own position, but any annoyance it may cause to Miss Prudence Manly, to whom we must address queries which you refuse to answer."

Higgins had walked back to the writing desk as though he had finished with the inspector. At these words he swung round in a blaze of sudden anger which he made no effort to rein.

"Prudence!" he exclaimed. "*Prudence!* You haven't been baiting her?"

"Then you admit that you know Miss Manly?"

"Know her? Of course I do. What the devil is that to you?"

"Miss Manly brought to our notice a document purporting to be a confession by Tucker Emmoll—a confession which might have very important consequences for yourself—which she said had been very strangely deposited in her own wood."

"In her *what*?"

"In her wood."

"I think one of us must be mad, if not more. How long is it since you heard this?"

"We've known it several days. If you had come with me at once instead of arguing here, it is possible that by now you might be hearing Miss Manly's account of the matter from her own mouth."

"You don't mean to say—you mean that you've got her at your infernal police station now?"

"It is quite likely that she'll be there."

"I can't believe that, unless you've arrested her too. And even your thick-headed British police couldn't be fools enough to think she'd murder anyone. As a matter of fact, she's due to meet me in about ten minutes now."

"She may have seen sufficient reason to alter her plans."

It was another shot in the dark, the inspector not having had the benefit of Superintendent Davis' conversation with Miss Manly, but it was likely enough. In any case, he felt that he had been justified in the line he had taken, for Mr. Higgins was pulling on his coat with an impatience that missed the armhole, and defeated his own haste. He had admitted his acquaintance with Miss Manly—and suppose that she should have preferred to deny it? He knew where she could be found, and, if she had declined to come to Scotland Yard, there might still be time to get in touch with her at the place where they had arranged to meet. He had not reacted quite as the inspector would have thought most likely, but he was obviously no ordinary criminal. He might even have been anticipating the possibility of such an inquisition, and have prepared his part in advance. These instantaneous thoughts were broken by Higgins' impatient voice: "Can't you get a move on, now that I've said I'll come? I suppose you've got a car outside? If not, you'd better come in a taxi with me."

"If you said you were coming, it was something I didn't hear. Yes, I've got a car waiting outside."

They went out together without further words passing the wide-eyed curiosity of Piggie Willing and three of the hotel staff, and were driven rapidly away.

Inspector Combridge, going over the conversation he had just had, got no farther than the reflection he had made many times in the past week: "It's about the craziest case I ever had."

# CHAPTER X.

INSPECTOR COMBRIDGE led the way to a bare-walled room containing little furniture, beyond a heavy table and chairs of equal stolidity. "You'd better wait here," he said, "while I let Superintendent Davis know."

But Higgins replied before he could reach the door: "I don't want to wait here. I must know at once. Unless Miss Manly—"

"I don't think Superintendent Davis will keep you waiting. He'll probably see you at once."

"But that's not the point. I want to know whether you've got Miss Manly here. If you haven't, she's meeting me, and I shall be late as it is. I didn't come here to—" He checked himself with the realization that loss of temper might not be the best way to the end he sought. "I beg your pardon," he said, "but you see how I'm placed, not knowing—"

The inspector, who did not doubt that Superintendent Davis was waiting to hear what luck he'd had, and who sought no more delay than would enable him to make report, answered equably: "I can't tell you what I don't know. I'm going to find out now, and I'll be back in three or four minutes, or perhaps a bit less than that."

He went out without giving time for further words, and was quickly in the Superintendent's room.

"Jibbed more than a bit," he said laconically, "but I've got him here. Had to mention Miss Manly, which I tried not to, and when I said she might be here, he changed his tune, and came at a run."

"He admitted knowing her?"

"Yes. But not about the confession. He said someone must be mad when I talked about that, so I shut up at once. I thought you'd like me to leave that to you. But it was the idea that we might be pumping her that set his legs moving in this direction. I hope you've persuaded her to come, or there'll be violence in about three minutes if we don't let him out."

"She'll be here almost at once now. But we'd better see her alone first. She may give us a different tale. You'd better tell him she isn't here yet, but we'll let him know when she comes."

Inspector Combridge went back to the waiting room on this errand, and pacified Higgins with a discreetly worded assurance that Miss Manly was certainly coming, would soon be there, and that he should see her when she did arrive. Ten minutes afterwards Miss Prudence Manly, having taken a taxi at Marylebone, appeared, inquired for Superintendent Davis, as she had been instructed to do, and was shown straight to his room.

She showed no sign, to that officer's shrewd and experienced eyes, of being nervously concerned as to the cause of her visit, and she appeared to have put aside whatever annoyance she may have felt at having been required to break her own engagement.

She greeted Inspector Combridge with a quiet cordiality, and accepted the superintendent's noncommittal handshake with the indifferent coolness of one to whom his grades of affability were of no concern.

"I think, in the first place, Miss Manly," he began, "you will like to know that we got in touch with Mr. Higgins this afternoon, and that he has come here. You'll be able to see him in a few minutes, when you have cleared up one or two points with me which seem to need further elucidation."

It seemed to him to be a judicious and even generous opening, giving her an opportunity for frankness after she had been told— perhaps warned would be a more appropriate word—that Edward Higgins had been found, and might already have been interrogated. Her reply did not suggest that she intended to take advantage of the opportunity in a spirit likely to win approbation from the official mind.

"You mean," she said, "that he was in England as well as his father? If that paper means that he'll be able to claim the estate, we must hope he's a better man."

"We're not sure about that. But the fact is, Miss Manly, that we want to give you an opportunity of doing yourself justice, and of hearing any further explanation you have to offer concerning the way in which the paper was found. In view of what we now know, it appears to us to be a most singular thing that it should have been placed where it was."

"It seemed a singular thing to me. But it was a fact, all the same. I suppose," she added, with a smile of characteristic humour, "you're not going to suggest that it wasn't there?"

"It is a serious—it may become a very serious matter, Miss Manly. I believe it is your own statement that you felt considerable hesitation in reporting the existence of the document to us."

"Yes, I did."

"May I ask why?"

"I've explained that already to Inspector Combridge. He made it the subject of one of his longer notes."

"May I suggest that the real reason was that you saw it might lead to the disclosure of your relationship to Edward Higgins?"

Miss Manly looked blank, and then amused. "I think," she said, "you are making a rather absurd mistake. So far as I'm aware I'm not related to Edward Higgins in the remotest degree."

"I didn't mean blood-relationship. Perhaps it's only fair to tell you that Mr. Higgins has admitted the position, which we had already learned from another source."

"What position?"

"Your previous acquaintance with and engagement to him."

"My *what*?" Miss Manly's laughter did not suggest the attitude of a woman about to be convicted of a foolish duplicity if not of more serious and probably criminal turpitude. "And you say you have him here now? May I see the gentleman?"

"Yes. I think you should. Combridge, we'll have Mr. Higgins in."

Superintendent Davis said this with his usual courtesy and with more than usual good humour. He was far from sure where the truth lay, and his experience inclined him, as it had inclined Inspector Combridge, to regard Miss Manly as unlikely to have involved herself in the meshes of sordid crime. Still, when a woman falls in love with a younger man—as the most austere of spinsters are apt to do!—he knew that strange consequences may result, and especially so if the object of such belated fall into peril of the criminal law. He delayed opinion of Miss Manly's veracity, but he felt that there was falsehood somewhere, and he knew that when those who are questioned resort to lies, it usually means that the truth is near.

\* \* \* \* \* \* \*

Higgins entered the room. He looked round, and his glance passed over Superintendent Davis, leaning back at his desk, and dwelt somewhat longer upon Miss Manly. There was no sign of recognition from the woman whom he had expressed such eagerness to meet, and who was looking at him with a most direct, though scarcely affectionate glance.

Miss Manly was first to speak. "Is this Mr. Higgins?" she asked.

Superintendent Davis, observing the blankness of the faces of the couple, looked interrogation at Inspector Combridge, who answered the unspoken question: "Yes, sir. There's no doubt about that." He was equally puzzled, but he remembered the signature in the hotel register—he considered the fact that a corresponding passport must have been produced—he recalled, most convincing of all, the conversation of the last hour.

"We have excellent reason," Superintendent Davis assured Miss Manly, "to believe it is."

"To the best of my recollection I have never seen the gentleman until now."

"What do you say, Mr. Higgins?"

But that gentleman looked at the lady who had denied his acquaintance, appeared about to speak, checked himself, and said nothing at all.

It was a silence with which the police officers could not be expected to remain content.

"Inspector Combridge tells me," the superintendent went on, "that you have already admitted your friendship with this lady, and that you only consented to come here when you learned that it would give you an opportunity of meeting her, for which you already had an appointment within the hour. After that, it seems useless to remain silent now."

"If he said anything of the kind, which is difficult to believe," Miss Manly interposed with uncompromising bluntness, "it was untrue. I repeat that I am not aware that I ever met him before."

"What have you to say, Mr. Higgins?"

"I—I don't want to say anything."

"But you have said it already. You are making matters no better for Miss Manly, and much worse for yourself, by this foolish attitude."

"The folly was that I came here at all. I'll go now, if you please. I've told you I sail tonight, and I've got a good deal to do."

"All the same, you can't go at present. I am not prepared to say that I can release you. Your attitude places you under a grave suspicion in regard to the murder of the man who appears to have confessed that he was your father. It obliges me to caution you that anything you say may be used in evidence, and you are not bound to say anything. But if you are an innocent man you have everything to gain by admitting, if it be true, that you are already acquainted with Miss Manly, or explaining how you came to make such an assertion, if it be false."

"You won't get anything more out of me. I've said too much already, and I wish I'd not been such a fool to talk at all."

The superintendent's glance moved to Miss Manly, who was regarding the man who had claimed to be affianced to her, and now refused either to repeat or deny it. He said "Miss Manly, I should like to believe what you say, especially as Mr. Higgins will not maintain his previous assertion now that he is confronted with you, but there is a great difficulty. I will be frank with you—franker, I'm afraid, than you are with me—and show you this cablegram which reached us shortly before I phoned you this afternoon. You will, I am sure, appreciate the significance of the fact that it was dispatched to us without any knowledge of the finding of the document which—if its genuineness be admitted—may confer a fortune upon Mr. Higgins."

Miss Manly took the cablegram without appearing to be greatly impressed, but she read it with an increased gravity. She looked up at Higgins, as though seeking explanation from a survey of that now angry and sullen man. She took a second look at the cablegram, which should not have taken long to read, and looked at Edward Higgins again with a puzzled scrutiny. It seemed to the keenly watching police officers that their eyes met in an understanding difficult to reconcile with the assertion that they were not previously acquainted.

Yet Miss Manly's next words showed that she was resolved to maintain that position in the absence of explanation, and in defiance of the inherent improbabilities which it involved.

She handed back the cablegram, saying with a quiet finality: "It is a most curious business from first to last. But I can only tell you again that I had not met Mr. Higgins, or even heard of him, until I read his name on the document from which all the trouble comes. I can't help wishing now that I hadn't brought it to your notice at all."

"That," the superintendent replied, "would have been a breach of your duty as a citizen, and might have been held to constitute a criminal offense."

"Then, if you consider that I had no option but to do that, and as that is the only act by which I had come into contact with these matters at all, I do not appear to be reasonably subject to further criticism from your department. I'm glad to have your approval of the course I took. But the matter is one with which I had no desire to be associated, and which I shall be glad to forget."

She rose as she spoke, drawing on her gloves, with the air of one who rejects a matter with which she is resolved to have no further concern. But Superintendent Davis, as though not observing the action, went on in his quietly deliberate manner:

"I'm sorry, Miss Manly, but we can't dismiss it quite as easily as you might like us to do. We've got to ask ourselves whether it really was planted in that wood as Inspector Combridge found it, or, rather, whether it was placed there by someone who was in collusion with you."

"You may ask yourselves any question you please," Miss Manly replied, with more sharpness in her voice than they had heard previously, "but as I've already told you all I know of the matter, you'll gain nothing further by asking me."

"I'm sorry to have to say it, Miss Manly, but I don't think you have."

The lady, ignoring this retort, turned to the door. "I suppose," she said, observing that Inspector Combridge, who was nearest, made no motion to open it, "I can find my own way out."

The inspector's eyebrows rose in silent interrogation, and gaining a slight nod in response, he opened the door for the angry lady. Seeing the way clear before her, she paused, and addressed Superintendent Davis with a resumption of her normal manner: "I believe that, while you have discovered the advantages of employing policewomen in the lower branches of your profession, they are still barred from the higher ranks. It must place you at a serious disadvantage in the investigations which you pursue."

"As for instance—?" Superintendent Davis queried amiably, wishing to encourage her to the possible indiscretion of further speech.

"Because the dullest woman would have taken about two minutes to guess the truth. And don't you think it's about time you let this young man go to his boat?"

Superintendent Davis replied with unperturbed good humour: "I wouldn't say you're far wrong about that. But I don't think Mr. Higgins is likely to sail tonight."

Miss Manly passed out through the door which Inspector Combridge was now holding open.

# CHAPTER XI.

INSPECTOR COMBRIDGE was polite enough to accompany Miss Manly to the pavement, and to overhear her instructions to the driver of the taxi which had promptly drawn up at the sign of his lifted hand. "Paddington. I want to catch the 7:20, so there's time enough without hurrying."

He knew that the Seer Green line is served by both Marylebone and Paddington stations, and he concluded soundly enough that she had no thought in her mind beyond getting home by the first available train. He had already decided that it would be a wise precaution to exercise supervision over her movements and correspondence, but that was a matter which there was time enough to arrange, and could best be done by a telephone instruction to the local police. At the moment, he was most concerned to get back to the room where Edward Higgins might, he thought, be persuaded to talk somewhat differently.

It was true that Miss Manly had given the driver his instructions without thought of duplicity, nor did she change them subsequently. She was, indeed, unpracticed in the subterfuges and intrigues which are common alike to those who serve and those who avoid the law. A severe disciplinarian of her own conscience, her first thought, as she reviewed the surprising interview from which she had come, was a doubt of whether she had been justified in her declaration that it would be useless to question her further, as she had already told all she knew. Well perhaps it was. Certainly, all she knew. All she guessed, or feared? Scarcely that. Indeed, her surmise approximated so clearly to certainty that she was disposed to blame herself for the indiscretion of her final jibe. She knew it had been her fault from childhood that she would say too much when tempted to the use of her own wit. Had she done so now? Probably it would make no difference, even if she had been understood, which she thought likely enough, for she had formed the opinion that the two police officers were exceptionally intelligent men. She saw that if her guess were right, the truth was not likely to remain longer concealed.

For, improbable as it seemed, the significance of what she had heard was beyond reasonable doubt. There was much that was mystery still—how she wished she knew!—the hand that had deposited the document in her grounds—the guilt or innocence of Edward Higgins, to which she had been so indifferent an hour before, and which might now be momentous to those nearest to her—well, that was beyond her deciding now. But one thing was certain. Edward Higgins had had an appointment to meet Prudence Manly and that appointment was not with her. Thinking of this, and of where such a meeting would be most likely to be arranged, the idea of catching the 7:20 left her mind. The taxi drew up at the Paddington pavement and she got out, entered the station, and began a systematic search of the waiting rooms.

In a corner of the large tea room which faces the arrival platforms, she saw a girl sitting at a small table alone. She drew back into the entrance, so that she could not be seen from where the girl sat, and stood there for some moments in unaccustomed irresolution, as though unprepared for the interview she had gone to so much trouble to gain. Finally, she went out, observed a telephone booth which was so placed that she could occupy it without losing sight of the refreshment room door, entered it, dialled the operator, and was soon put through to a Marlow number.

"That you, Tabitha? Yes, Prudence. I'm speaking from Paddington. Yes, so did I. But I didn't go. I came to town unexpectedly. Oh, business. Rather annoying, but I'll tell you about that next time I see you. I've got Prudence here now. I hope you won't mind if I take her home with me for the night. No, he didn't turn up. Well, him or her! I didn't ask her."

The conversation concluded with some exchanges of little interest except to the two who spoke, and which Miss Manly was inclined to cut as short as good manners to a sister-in-law more garrulous than herself would allow. She feared that the conversation might revert at any moment to a subject for which the time and place would be inopportune for a full confidence, and concerning which she would be reluctant to lie.

Having done this, she returned to the tea room and advanced straight to the table where the girl sat without observing her approach; for though the girl had come to meet a lover who was provokingly late, she had ceased, after an hour's waiting, to look round for one who did not appear. She had no need to watch for fear he might overlook her if his attention were not attracted. It was a place where they had met before, and she was in the corner seat which they were accustomed to choose. Even the long waiting would not have greatly perturbed her mind but for the fact that there was the hour of her return to watch, and the time available for this last meeting was shortening ominously. But Edward had said that he might have much to do on his last day in England. He would be there as punctually as he could—she had no doubt of that!—and she was not to worry if he should be later than she. Now she sat hardly conscious of where she was, as her mind went over the plans they had discussed a few days before, which were to be defined and agreed upon tonight.

She raised expectant eyes, which changed to bewilderment, as she saw who it was who pulled back the vacant chair and sat down at the other side of the little table.

Miss Manly drew off her gloves. "I don't often come in here," she said. "I prefer getting my meals at home. But when I saw you—"

The troubled dark-blue eyes were veiled for a moment by darker lashes, and when they were seen again their owner had regained control of herself.

"You startled me," she answered, with the welcoming smile which a favourite niece should give to an aunt whom she has found reason to trust. "Mother told me you were going to the Bensons' this evening."

"So I was," she said; "but I had a rather urgent request to call at the police office at Scotland Yard to explain a cable they had received from New York."

"From New York!" The exclamation was one of faint surprise, but the fact was that Prudence Manly, the younger, was giving little more than outward attention to what she heard. How—with what excuse—could she get her aunt to go in the speediest, most natural way? When was the next train? Should she risk leaving the place of rendezvous herself, or of Edward Higgins finding them together? What explanation should she give when her aunt should ask, as in the next moment she surely must, what was her reason for sitting there? But Miss Manly's next words wakened her to an actuality more formidable than her fears.

"Yes. From New York. It said that I was engaged to a Mr. Tucker Higgins, a son, as he claims to be, of the Tucker Emmoll who was murdered in Jordans."

"That *you* were? But how absurd! And I don't see why—"

The startled exclamations of a genuine astonishment covered for a moment a quick-witted consideration of how much must have been disclosed; how much, if anything, might still be left concealed and unguessed; how far, if her aunt had discovered all, could she hope to give confidence and win sympathy from her?

"I suppose," she went on, puzzling over a connecting link which she could not see, "it was because you live at Jordans, and it happened there."

"There was more in it than that. Someone put a paper in the wood which seems to be a confession by the man who was killed that Edward Higgins is his son."

"You mean in *your* wood?"

"Yes. On the path. Under an old umbrella."

"But what on earth would make them do that?"

"That's more than I can say. The police evidently thought I'd had something to do with putting it there, even if I hadn't forged it in the hope of getting a fortune for the man I was proposing to marry."

"Will it? They couldn't really be silly enough to think you'd do things like that! I mean, will it really make him a rich man?"

"I should think it would depend upon whether it proves to be a genuine document, and then upon whether his father had made a will before he was killed, or killed himself, as it seems to say that he did."

"We know he didn't do that."

Conscious of her aunt's surprise at the definiteness of this assertion, the girl went on: "Of course that was plain enough from what was in the papers." And then she asked bluntly: "What did the police say when you told them it wasn't true?"

"They probably thought more than they said. But they didn't seem to guess the truth. I left them discussing the matter with Mr. Higgins."

"You mean they've got hold of him?" There was alarm in the girl's voice now. "What did he say? They're not going to make any trouble for him? I don't see what he's got to do with it at all."

"I don't know that he has, and I don't thing they do. But the document being found in Prudence Manly's wood, and hearing that he is engaged to someone of that name, they naturally think it is a very singular coincidence and wonder whether he or I had any part in putting it there, and, of course, how we got hold of it, if we did."

"It does seem strange. I suppose you don't know who really did? But you don't think it will mean any trouble for him?"

"I should think it will depend upon how far they think he's been frank with them. Though of course I don't know how far he can afford to be that, the gentleman being a stranger to me."

"He didn't tell them anything—of course I can see that you guess what a mess I'm in!—he didn't tell them anything about me?"

"No. You weren't mentioned. Of course, it's bound to come out. I mean the police will find out what the truth is, unless they're absolute fools, and they didn't strike me that way. But I don't think your Mr. Higgins meant to help them."

The girl rose from her seat. "I don't want him to get into any trouble for that. You say he's at Scotland Yard now? I think I'd better go."

But Miss Manly kept her seat, and replied: "I don't think you had. I think you'll be a very silly girl if you do. Suppose he's refused to admit that you exist, and you walk in and show them he's been telling lies? Is that going to do him good?"

"But he was sailing tonight!"

"I doubt whether he will now. But if he is, he'll probably have left Scotland Yard, and you'd miss him there, and just make fresh trouble for him for nothing. What you'd better do is to come home with me, and we'll decide what's best to be done when I understand a bit more than I do now. There may still be time when we get home to find out by telephone whether he's on the boat."

"I think—I don't like to leave it like that—I think I'd much rather go."

"But what could you hope to do? You might do harm, but I don't see how you could do any good. *Unless you really know something about how that paper got where it did.*"

"No. How could I? I haven't the least idea."

"Then I'm sure you'd better come with me now."

"But Mother—she thinks I'm meeting—well, she doesn't really know who. I promised to be home on the 9:13."

"I've telephoned her already to say you're coming with me tonight."

"You've—? Then you must have known it all the time?"

"I didn't know. But it was very easy to guess."

"What did you tell Mother?"

"I didn't tell her anything. It's for you to do that."

"I suppose she'll have to know now. What a mess it is! You don't think Edward's in any real trouble?"

"I'm afraid I don't know enough about him to answer that. But if he's done nothing wrong, he's not likely to have much to fear."

"He hasn't killed people, or made up papers, if you mean that."

"I didn't say he had. But you see he was a stranger to me up to about two hours ago."

"If you've seen him, I should have thought that would be enough."

"Perhaps it ought to have been. I certainly don't want to think he's done anything wrong."

Miss Manly said this with an emphasis which silenced the younger woman. She spoke with sincerity. Certainly she did not wish to think evil of one of whom her niece was fond. But inclination and conviction are different matters. She recognized the reasonableness of the police view, even as it glanced at herself. And knowledge of her own innocence did nothing to explain the mystery of why her wood had been selected for the deposit of the document from which this trouble had come. Beyond that, it was a fact that Tucker Emmoll was dead, and that suspicion, so far as she knew, attached to no one else as it must attach to the putative son who had followed him to England, and who had so deep a cause to seek revenge. And there was the secrecy and evasion with which his relations with her niece had developed, for which she saw no adequate reason, and which was natural to resent.

But she was not one to judge before the witnesses had been heard, and she had little doubt that she would know the truth before midnight came.

On arriving home, she rang up the offices of the steamship lines and learned that Edward Higgins was not sailing that night, and that his baggage had been removed from the boat. But, for neither woman, was there any great comfort in that.

\* \* \* \* \* \* \*

Inspector Combridge went back to Superintendent Davis' room—after assuring himself that Miss Manly was returning to Paddington, and drawing inaccurate conclusions therefrom—and found that officer alone. He asked, in some natural surprise: "You haven't let Higgins go?"

"No. But I thought I'd give him a quiet half-hour to think it over. There'll still be time to run him down to his boat, if he has the sense to come clean, and if we hear a tale that justifies us in letting him go. But I don't think we shall. Whether he talks or not, I reckon we shall want a little more of his company than we've had yet. Do you think we're really as dense as that woman said?"

"Oh, I don't know that I'd differ much about that. I haven't ever felt very bright over this case, and I don't now. We keep finding fresh facts, but they don't get us any farther that I can see. Not in the way we want to go."

"You haven't done badly so far. And you were right about Miss Manly. The question is, was she right about us? I suppose you saw what she meant?"

"No. I can't say that I did. I've hardly given it a thought. But I'm glad you agree with me that she's straight, however unlikely it may have seemed."

"What she meant was, that she isn't the Prudence Manly to whom this fellow we've got here is engaged. Of course, it's a younger woman. Probably a cousin or niece. We ought to have thought of that."

"I don't see why we should. Not before we'd seen them together."

"We know the age of Tucker Emmoll's son."

Inspector Combridge recognized the probability of this explanation, but with more concern for its contribution towards the elucidation of a baffling problem than as to whether the charge of natural masculine stupidity could be established against him. He said: "It looks as though she didn't mind giving us the straight tip. I'm glad you've put Higgins back for a time. I'll try to get those dates he was away from his hotel before we talk to him again."

He went off to a telephone in another room, and came back in ten minutes with a sheet of paper on which he had jotted down some dates and a line of verse.

"I don't think we've got much farther to look," he said, "for the man—one of the men, anyway—who did Emmoll in. Higgins was away from Willing's Hotel three nights in the beginning of January—that's when he's supposed to have gone to Glasgow on business—and four nights later, and these last are in the last week of the month. The night that Emmoll was killed, and the next three after that.

"He didn't go anywhere by train on that occasion. Piggie Willing's done some quick work for us about that. The porter remembered hearing something from a friend of his at Page's garage about Higgins having hired a car for a month and taken it back after a few days. So Willing rang them up, and he finds that's just what he did. He hired a big saloon car—a Morris-Oxford, maroon—and returned it late on the fourth night. It seems—and this is the only point that's in his favour at all—that he wanted a smaller car, but they let him have that one cheap, because all their lighter ones were in use and there's not so much demand for the heavy cars.

"The other thing I've got hold of—and it's not so easy to see what it's worth to us—is one of his silly lines. It doesn't make any sense that I can see, but anyway, here it is."

With these words, Inspector Combridge, as though reluctant to descend to the reading of such puerilities, passed the paper over to his superior officer, who read:

*"Too faint the heart that in you lies the debt of life to dare."*

"They say," Inspector Combridge went on, "that it's scrawled several times on a sheet of paper that he tore up and threw away, after he'd written it two or three different ways. But that's how it seems to have settled down. He put 'cold' instead of 'faint' and another word before that, and the first time he wrote it he just left a blank where he put 'heart' later on."

"Poetry," Superintendent Davis replied, wishing to treat the subject in a more liberal spirit, "isn't expected to have much sense. It's like music. It's the sound that counts, not the words."

"Well, it's sense we want," Inspector Combridge replied. "The sound won't be much good to us. And when a man writes the end of a sentence before he's made up his mind what the beginning's to be, we're not likely to get much of that. Unless he put something in the waste-paper basket about how he was going to do the crime. I don't see that it gets us much farther than showing that both he and the man who murdered his father had a habit of making rhymes. So many persons are rhymesters."

"But what," Superintendent Davis, who had been giving concentrated attention to the latter half of the line, asked in a less querulous spirit, "do you make of 'the debt of life to dare'?"

"I don't make anything of it. It hasn't got any meaning. Not in any English I ever learned."

"You don't think it might mean something about taking the risk that he might be hanged?"

Inspector Combridge saw a possibility here which prejudice must not allow him to overlook. He considered the line again. "Then," he said, "if that was it, why didn't he say it straight out, and not make so much trouble for us? It makes me sick when a man can't write what he means. But there may be something in that. Something that a good counsel could use."

He imagined Denis Hartlin talking to a jury about that line for half an hour till there would be nothing clear in their bewildered minds beyond the fact that Edward Higgins had written a poem about the crime before he went forth to slay. He added: "Well, I'd better see what we've got on the records about Morris-Oxfords. A bit of help there, and you might say we're well on the homeward track. About time, too, I fancy."

He went away again, and in a short time he returned with three letters which had been received from people who had seen a Morris-Oxford saloon car acting, they said, in a suspicious manner on the night, and more or less in the neighbourhood of the crime. Two of those were definite that the car was maroon in colour, and the third thought it was a dark blue.

"This all?" Superintendent Davis asked, as the three letters were passed over to him.

"Yes. There were forty-eight people who wrote to us about cars they had seen doing funny things in the night, but they're mostly the wrong kind. There was one more that might have done us a bit of good if the man hadn't said that he was nearly sure that it was a Morris and quite sure that it was a light gray."

"Well, three ought to do. Enough's as good as a feast, if they'll tell the tale in the right way."

"I'll have them looked up tomorrow."

Inspector Combridge had denied with sincerity that a case is ever "framed" against an accused person by the English police. But he would have found it difficult to deny, in such details as this, that the preparation of a case for trial involves a process of selection, elimination, and adaptation, in the course of which much contradictory evidence is molded into a form which will be likely both to convince a jury and satisfy legal rules.

The evidence of the three letter-writers would be much more convincing when considered alone than in conjunction with the testimony of forty-five others who had been equally suspicious of different cars. It would inevitably gain in unity of presentation as it would be rehearsed with the observant three, and the rough edges of discrepancy smoothed away. Yet, in such procedure, there would be no aiming at injustice, and no probability that injustice would result.

Besides, did it logically follow that the three were not telling what they had seen, because forty-five others had observed various other things?

"I suppose," Combridge said, "we'd better have Higgins back now. Suppose he can give a satisfactory account of what he was doing during those four nights?"

"It isn't likely; but, even so, we'll be justified in detaining him until we have some confirmation of whatever he says. And after that there would be the question of how that document came to be in Miss Manly's garden. Even if we find that there's another Prudence, as he may admit now he's had time for a little thought, it still remains just as probable as before—perhaps more so—that it was he who put it where it was found. And how did it come into his hands? If he can explain that too, he has a chance to get clear, but I should say it's about the toughest job that a wriggling murderer ever had."

"He won't do much expert wriggling. He's too quick-tempered for that. I should say he's more likely to blurt it all out and say that he only gave Emmoll what he deserved."

"He won't do much good for himself if he pleads that."

"No. But he may make a bad guess. In his own country, he'd have a chance. Emphasis on always having been a good son, and avenging his mother's wrongs."

"Well, we'll have him in again, and we'll soon know where we are, better than we do now. Have Sergeant Bates sitting by, in case we get Higgins in the right mood for making a statement."

This prudent arrangement having been made, Higgins was brought back into the room. He was now accompanied by two burly constables. It would not have been surprising had the black anger in his eyes been translated into a torrent of wrathful words, but he restrained himself until he had ascertained what his captors proposed to do. If they decided to let him go, there might still be time to return to the hotel, and from there to King George V Dock. Time, even, to rush round to Paddington station and see Prudence But it was a hope that ended with the first words he heard.

"We have considered the position," Superintendent Davis began, with his usual deliberation, "and while we shall be obliged to detain you for a short time to enable us to verify whatever explanation you may wish to give, I want you to understand that you are not at present charged. Also that we're prepared to consider such explanations, and that, if they should prove satisfactory, you will be free to go.

"But I have also to warn you that you are under very grave suspicion in more than one particular. You are under no obligation to say anything, if you prefer to remain silent, and anything that you do say may be used in evidence, if a charge should be subsequently made."

It was with an evident effort at self-control that Higgins gave a quiet reply. "I've told you already that I'm absolutely innocent of the murder of Tucker Emmoll. I know nothing whatever about it, beyond what I read in the newspapers. And I've had nothing to do with any paper he signed, and I never heard of it till you came to me this afternoon. I haven't refused to answer any questions you've asked, except when they've been on matters that don't concern you in any way. And I'm glad to see you've got someone taking this down, and you're free to use it against me in any way that you can.

"I should like to add that I want a plain answer to the question, am I arrested or am I not? If you say no, I should like to know what will happen if I walk out of here, as, if I am not under arrest, I suppose I must have the right to do. Ah, I thought that might stop his pen!"

The last exclamation came as he observed that Sergeant Bates had paused in his shorthand, and was looking at his superior officers in some doubt of whether this question were to be entered on the record. But Superintendent Davis said shortly: "Got that, Bates?" As the pen resumed its activity, he answered easily: "You are not arrested, and you are not charged, but you are detained on suspicion. Whether you will be charged or released in the next few hours will depend mainly on whether you are able to give satisfactory explanations on certain points, some of which have been put to you already."

"So far as I can see you've got nothing against me at all, and you're trying to get me to answer questions in the hope that you'll get something by that means. I've got nothing guilty to hide, and unless you ask private things that have nothing to do with the matter, I don't mind answering anything. But, all the same, I protest against being kept here when I've booked my passage and the boat's sailing tonight."

"Very well. Got that, Bates? You have a note that Mr. Higgins protests? Now, Mr. Higgins, do you still decline to admit that you are engaged to Miss Prudence Manly?"

"I am not engaged to the lady you had here."

"Possibly not. But to another of the same name?"

"I decline to answer, because the question can have no connection with your investigation of Tucker Emmoll's murder."

"Very well. You decline. You only put us to a little further trouble in finding it out in our own way. Do you also refuse to tell us where you were on the night of the murder?"

"I suppose I was at the hotel."

"And we happen to know you were not. You were driving about that night in a Morris-Oxford car. I'm treating you as fairly as I can when I tell you we know that already. If you've got any proper explanation of what you were doing in it, we're here to listen."

The statement appeared to reduce Higgins to a condition of dumb confusion very different from the confident, defiant attitude of the moment before. He said at last: "I don't say I wasn't, if that happened to be the date. But I wasn't murdering Tucker Emmoll, if you mean that. It was just a coincidence that I was away from the hotel that night. You can't make much of that."

"We don't want to make anything of it, if you can show us how you were properly occupied during that and the two following nights."

"I wasn't in London at all, nor in Buckinghamshire. I was away on business of my own in quite another part of the country."

"That being—?"

"I'm not prepared to say more than that."

"You mean you won't say where you were?"

"Yes. I mean that, I was away on business that concerns no one but myself."

"Then I have no further questions to ask."

Higgins was led away to the cells, and the two officers were left alone to consider the position created by the repeated and angry denials which they had heard.

"He didn't expect," Inspector Combridge said, "that we should have found out about the car."

"No, it took him rather aback."

"But I should call him a clever liar, considering the hole he's in. He's far better off than if he'd invented an explanation that he couldn't sustain."

"The question you've got to consider now is whether you've got enough evidence for a committal."

"I've got enough for a remand, and when I've got that, I ought to be able to get the thing into shape."

Inspector Combridge spoke with reasonable confidence. His experience was that when he got the right man into the cells, with as much evidence as he now had, there was seldom much difficulty in establishing further facts. But he had had a hard day. Tomorrow he would tackle the case again with a fresher mind.

# CHAPTER XII.

"THE fact is," Miss Manly said, when she had ascertained that Edward Higgins was not leaving England that night, as she had still hoped, both for her niece's sake and her own, "the fact is that we're both about starved, and we're not fit to talk about anything till we've had a good meal."

She was conscious that she had tasted nothing since lunch, and she correctly supposed her niece to be in a similar condition. The nature of their conversation at Paddington had caused them both to ignore the natural use of the tea room in which it had been held.

Now they sat down to a dinner which, if not luxurious, was well-cooked and well-served, and no less welcome to them because it had been held back for over two hours.

The younger Prudence made no objection to a respite which gave her time to rehearse events and range excuses for the confession which she saw now had become an unescapable ordeal. Her aunt, guessing more or less what it was certain to be, was not sorry for an equal pause to consider in what manner it would be wisest that it should be received.

It was only when they had moved to the lounge, and settled themselves into a fireside seat that the girl began abruptly: "I suppose you think I've done something dreadful?"

"No. I'm sure you wouldn't do anything that I should describe by that word."

The girl was silent, wishing she were equally sure, and her aunt added: "But I daresay you've done something that wasn't wise, and evidently something which you have concealed from your parents, because you don't expect them to approve."

"No," she said with conviction, "they won't approve. But the way things went I don't see how I could—not without making trouble that would do nobody good."

"Are you going to tell me that you've made a mistake, or that you still think you did the right thing?"

"I don't say everything was exactly right. Oh, I know I'm in a horrible mess! But I'm not going to give Edward up, if you mean that."

"Perhaps you'd better tell me from the beginning. I suppose you met Mr. Higgins when you were with Constance last year?"

Miss Manly remembered, as she asked this, that when Prudence had been invited to accompany a school friend on a three months' holiday in the States, it was by her own advocacy that it had been arranged.

"Yes. Of course. I met him first at the Melsons', in New York, and we—we fell in love all at once."

"Well, I daresay that was natural enough. But why shouldn't anyone be allowed to know all about it?"

"He's a Catholic, for one thing. You know what Mother'd say about that."

It was not what Miss Manly had expected to hear, and seemed a redundant jest of adverse circumstance, thrown into an already over-weighted scale. But she recognized that its separate gravity was sufficient. Yes, she knew what Tabitha would say about that!

"It's a pity," the girl went on, "that people get so bigoted about what they believe. It makes a lot of trouble that needn't happen."

"It's a pity anyone's bigoted," the older woman answered, unwilling either to endorse or condemn her sister-in-law's prejudice.

"Well, he didn't mind marrying me."

"Nor you him, as it appears." She was on the point of asking whether his own parents might not have had an equal objection, when she remembered that the father had been an absent and even doubtful quantity, and the mother might have been fully occupied in another way. She asked, more vaguely: "Was there any difficulty other than this matter of religion?"

"Yes. I suppose there was. I mean, not really, but you know how Mother'd have felt. I mean about Edward having his mother's name, and about her going to prison, and all that. You can't wonder that Edward hated his father."

Yes, again she saw how Tabitha would have felt. She didn't like it herself. She understood also how Edward might hate his father. But there was no comfort in that, seeing how it blackened the present suspicion under which he lay. But it was true also that, if it were a genuine document which she had found under that old umbrella, his mother's name was likely to be vindicated, and that there had been justification for what she did.

"I don't wonder at that," she said gently, "and as to going to prison, your great-grandfather was there for three weeks, because he wouldn't take his hat off in church. His brother was imprisoned for a much better action than that. It isn't being in prison that matters, it's why you're there."

"Oh, but that was a long time ago! Mother'd look at it very differently if it happened today."

This was again an indisputable proposition. There was no doubt that Tabitha would! But all this, serious as it might once have seemed, became an almost trivial background to the problem of the girl's entanglement with a possible murderer. A man of dubious character, and most dubious ancestry.

Miss Manly could not forget the problem of how that curious document of confession came to be planted in her own wood. Nor did she overlook the seriousness of the words with which this conversation commenced: "I'm not going to give Edward up, if you mean that." She saw the probability of unpleasant publicity; the possibility of some shameful sequel, easier to dread than define. She knew her niece's disposition, pliable but persistent. Not given to duplicity. Frank and straightforward under normal circumstances, and generous in all. But always disposed to take the line of least resistance towards that which she was resolved to have. She was silent for seconds, then asked: "Did Constance know this?"

"Yes. She had to. She readdressed his letters."

"You mean she sent them on to you under cover of envelopes she addressed herself."

"Yes. We had to do it that way. I didn't want to have to tell lies to Mother."

"And how did you think it was going to end?"

"I thought there'd be an awful row. But I thought that would be the best way in the end. I wanted Edward to come here, as he did, and then we'd have it out, and I'd get Mother to say yes if I could; but I meant to marry him whether or not."

"But if he agreed to that, I don't see why—"

"He didn't at first. When he got here, he wanted us to get married first, and tell them when it was done."

"You couldn't do that at your age. Not without your parents' consent, or at least their knowledge."

"Yes. I know that now. I'd just persuaded Edward to spill the beans—"

"To do what?"

"That's what he called it. To have it all out. Then his father got killed, and after that—well, you can see! So we agreed that he should go back, and I should go out to him next June, when I should be old enough to do what I want myself."

The girl became silent, until her aunt asked at last: "And that's the whole tale?"

"Yes. At least—yes, of course it's all. It's all, so far. What more is there to say?"

"Of course, you don't know anything about this queer document, or about—how his father died?"

"No. How should I? And they've no right to say that Edward does, either." The girl paused. Then, as though conscious that she had not answered in the most convincing manner, she added: "I haven't the least idea. Not the foggiest. I don't see why you think I should."

"I don't think so at all, if you say that," Miss Manly answered, "and in that way I'm glad it's no worse than it is."

99

She spoke sincerely, but—all the truth? She wished it were, but she had a doubt that she could not still.

The girl thought: "All the truth? How I wish it were!" But there was one thing which, even in that confidence, she would leave untold.

Inspector Combridge got up next morning with a feeling not unlike that of a business man who has the anxieties of many transactions upon his mind. There was much that must be seen to during the day. Much more to be done before he could hope to satisfy the Crown solicitors with the case which they would have to prepare. But such matters—such difficulties—are the routine of a detective-inspector's life, with which his superior officers expect him to be equal to deal.

With these thoughts, he reached the portals of Scotland Yard, and was promptly informed that Miss Prudence Manly had called up to speak to him, and asked to be called as soon as he should arrive.

"I am authorized by my niece, Prudence," Miss Manly said, "to let you know that it was she to whom the cable which you showed me yesterday afternoon referred."

"Thank you, Miss Manly. And her address is?"

"She is staying with me here."

"Do you mean that she resides with you permanently?"

"No. I asked her here last night to discuss the position which has arisen."

"I suppose I can see her? What address shall I use for that?"

"Do you think that is necessary?"

"I should certainly like to hear here account of the matter."

"Of what matter? You should understand that she is a young girl not yet of age, and it is very undesirable that she should be involved in legal matters of any kind."

"I am afraid the interests of justice must come before such considerations."

"I don't see what the interests of justice have to do with the matter. It isn't a criminal thing to have been engaged to a young man who subsequently gets into some trouble with you. Would you say that it is, Inspector?"

Inspector Combridge was not instant in his reply. He could not avoid seeing that there was some reason in Miss Manly's contention. He had in fact, nothing whatever against the younger Prudence, nor anything which connected her in the slightest degree with the crime for which her lover had been arrested. His desire to question her rose from the hope that she would say something which would assist him to construct a stronger case against Edward Higgins, and it was not a purpose which he could expect her to appreciate at his own value. All the same, he had no intention of giving way. His crop was too poor at present for him to abandon the ploughing of likely ground. And in the instant that his reply paused, Miss Manly's well-developed conscience accused her of having spoken rather from her own feelings than as her niece had requested, at which she added hastily:

"But we thought you ought to know, because it explains his real reason for coming to England. It should, I suppose, remove the suspicion you had yesterday when he refused to give an explanation which would have involved my niece in his own trouble. In fact, it makes it particularly improbable that he would allow himself to be involved in violence of any kind."

"I don't think it would serve any useful purpose to discuss that, Miss Manly; but I don't mind telling you that we've got a lot of evidence which all points the same way. I know you think we're mugs here, but—"

"I didn't say that, Inspector, and I hope you believe that I didn't mean it. I only commented, I hope fairly enough, on the fact that neither you nor Superintendent Davis seemed to recognize the probability that the cable might refer to a younger woman."

Inspector Combridge failed to observe the opening for compliment that this statement gave. He only said: "Well, you see you knew that you had a niece of that name, and we didn't."

"Will it be a serious breach of your regulations if I ask whether you were the cause of Mr. Higgins losing his boat last night, as I have some reason to think he did?"

"We have arrested Edward Higgins for the murder of Tucker Emmoll, and whatever we may do in regard to the young lady—and

I need scarcely say, Miss Manly, that we always try, as far as possible, to avoid causing any needless distress—we may have to ask you to give evidence."

"What about?"

"About the finding of the document in your wood."

"Do you mean that it was put there by Mr. Higgins?"

"I'm afraid I can't discuss that. All we shall ask you to do is to state what happened to your own knowledge."

"I am not likely to object to that. When will it be?"

"We'll let you know in good time. Probably a week from now. We shall do no more than take a remand today."

"I suppose the young man will be properly defended?"

"I'm sure he will be. They usually are. But he won't be needing much help today. It will be no more than a matter of keeping his mouth shut, and he doesn't seem to need any lessons in that."

"Well, thank you, Inspector. I've no doubt you think you have a good case, but I'm not so sure, and you'll forgive me for hoping you're wrong."

"We're not often wrong when we get as far as we have now."

At this point the conversation terminated.

At the hour of noon, Edward Higgins was brought before a police court magistrate, Prescott Elsworth, and made his first acquaintance with the more public aspects of the process of English law.

Magistrate Elsworth, whose fifteen years in a metropolitan court had taught him a wide tolerance and understanding of the criminal world, glanced with a shrewd but not unkindly curiosity at this alien prisoner and asked by whom he was represented.

Higgins answered from the dock that he did not wish to be represented at all. He preferred to defend himself.

Elsworth was troubled, even embarrassed, by this attitude. "It is highly unusual, and I think it unwise for you to dispense with expert legal advice. I must earnestly ask you in your own interests to reconsider your decision."

"Well, I've done nothing wrong, and I've got a tongue, and before I make up my mind whether I'll do my own talking, I think I'll hear what the frame-up's like." The magistrate frowned at this expression, the use of which strengthened his judgment that Edward Higgins was not equipped by nature or training for the conduct of his own defense.

"If you are without means," he said, "there is a provision of English law by which suitable legal assistance is made available."

"I haven't much money here. I ought to have sailed home last night. But I'm not exactly a pauper, if you mean that."

"It is a matter which I am sure could—which should be arranged." The magistrate's glance moved along the solicitor's bench, as though looking for one to whom he could confide the prisoner's interests to his own satisfaction, but before he spoke, Edward Higgins broke out again.

"If I agree to put up some money, will I get it back when the cops lay off me?"

"No. I can't say that you would."

"Then we'll skip it."

Elsworth did not profess ignorance of this colloquialism. For the moment, he appeared to accept the position. He turned to Blakeway, the prosecuting solicitor, to ask: "I suppose you won't want to go beyond a formal remand today?" Receiving an affirmative reply, he said: "Very well, we'll get on."

In less than five minutes Edward Higgins found that the proceedings were over, and he was back in a room which had a rather unpleasant odour, though it had the appearance of being kept scrupulously clean, and the plain solidity of its meagre furniture could do little to harbour dirt.

He had not been sitting in the room for more than a few minutes, his mind toying idly with the idea of a sudden rush, when a young man entered, greeted the sergeant in charge, and came over directly to where Higgins sat.

"I represent the *Sunday Mail*," he said briskly, offering a card. "Mr. Elsworth gave me permission to see you. We don't know whether you killed Emmoll or not, and of course I'm not going to ask—not now, anyway—but he wasn't much loss, if half of what we've raked up about him's a quarter true. We're sorry to see you in such a jam, and if the best counsel that cash can hire will get you out of the soup—well, we're ready to put it up."

"I suppose I needn't ask where the catch lies?"

"We only want a life history, which you can write for us, or just give us the details to write it up. It won't go to the press till the trial's done."

Higgins shook his head. "Nothing doing," he said.

"Well, if you don't do it yourself, you'll find others will, and it won't read any better for that. There's no harm in talking it over, and seeing just what it would mean."

"You'll waste your time if you do."

"Well, it's my time," the young man answered with an engaging smile. As he spoke he drew up one of the chairs with an ease of motion which suggested that previous practice had taught him just how heavy they were.

It was nearly half an hour later that he found a basis of bargaining to which this difficult murderer would respond. And twenty minutes later the whole length of Fleet Street knew that the Emmoll murderer had been cornered by the *Sunday Mail*, and that they must scavenge round for interviews with the minor characters in the coming drama, or for such details and photographs as were open for all to seize.

Inspector Combridge, meanwhile, after a hurried lunch, must attend a conference at Prosecutor Blakeway's office, where that gentleman, with two of his associates, reviewed the case as it stood.

"I don't doubt," Blakeway said, after nearly two hours of animated discussion, "that you've got the man. And I don't say you haven't done well to get as far as you have in about the queerest case I've had in this office. And in the last thirty years I've had more than a few.

"And you mustn't think I'm pessimistic; because you've got a clear week, and you've done so much already that I've no doubt with that extra time you'll have a much better case than you have now. But what I say is that you allowed yourselves to be rushed by the fact that the man was just going on board his ship, and you brought him in before the case was ready for dishing up. As it stands, it's got so many loose ends that it's hard even to guess what side a clever lawyer would choose to pull at to get you down.

"You can't say where the murder took place. You don't know anything about Emmoll's movements, or who he was with from the moment he left Marsden Terrace to when he's a stuck-up guy on the Jordans stile.

"You've got this queer document, and no idea as to how it came into existence, or whether it's genuine, or how it came to be where it was, and even if—"

"That's not quite correct," the inspector interposed. "I am inclined to think it's genuine and I think it's almost certain that Higgins planted it there."

"Then how do you get over the point that whoever wrote it was intending to take his own life?"

"I think," Inspector Combridge answered patiently, "that there are two possible explanations. One is that the document is only a clever copy of the original, and that sentence has been stuck in.

"I don't urge that theory, because it's probably in Emmoll's writing. Besides that, it's on the back of the hotel bill, which was certainly in his pocket when he left the hotel. But you must see that it's possible. Whatever he wrote may have been found, perhaps on later consideration, to have something in it which it wouldn't do to produce. And so, with the use of this hotel bill, which was in the clothes they'd stripped off him, and the genuine document to guide them, they make what I'll own to be one of the cleverest forgeries I ever saw in all my fairly wide experience.

"But a more probable and a much simpler theory is that it was written under compulsion, very likely with a gun-barrel poking into his back, and perhaps induced by some promise that wasn't kept."

"Yes. That may be a likely guess as far as it goes, but there's one point it doesn't reach. You want to set up that the son, bent on revenge and set on securing his inheritance, follows his father to this country, bullies him into signing this curious document, and then slowly bleeds him to death with a pocket knife, strips his body, and conveys it from wherever the murder took place to the Jordans stile, where he stuck the body up as it was found.

105

"Well, the answer to all that is that it couldn't be done. Not by one man, that is. And where would Higgins get an accomplice for such a crime?

"If you can't find the second man, I doubt whether there's a barrister at the bar who could persuade any jury to convict—and with the judge summing up in the way he'd be almost certain to do."

Inspector Combridge was plainly worried either by the logical strength of this argument, or by the force with which it was put by one on whom he must rely to prepare the case on the result of which the reputation of his department hung.

"You mustn't suppose," he said, "that I haven't considered that; but if there must have been an accomplice, well then there was one! And now we've got one of the men, the second ought to be a lot simpler to find. We've got a week, as you said, and it's often been long enough. We haven't quite put that young butcher out of the picture yet. Besides, there's the girl. It's not likely, I know. But we haven't seen what she's like, and she'd as much to gain as the man in getting Emmoll to write what it seems he did.

"Then I've got Higgins' baggage to go over. The sudden way we ran him in ought to leave a good chance of something useful in that. And—well, there are other directions where inquiries can be made, now that we can feel sure we're on the right scent. If you'll just go ahead and prepare a brief with the material you've already got, I think you can depend on a bit more before it's time to be worrying what a jury'll think."

"You think we can prepare a decent brief from what we've got now?"

"I think you make it out to be worse than it is. Motive and opportunity—we always reckon when we've got those that we are half-way home. And we've got them both in abundance here. There's more than casual opportunity. There's pursuit. Pursuit right across the world. And then hiring the car, and going off no one knows where on the night Emmoll gets killed.

"And then the place where he planted the paper—I know the way it came to our knowledge, and that cable at the same time, makes it seem crude. But it may have been very far from that.

"We saw that Miss Manly was an utter stranger to him. Suppose his intrigue with the girl was a secret that the two thought nobody knew? Wouldn't it be rather neat to bring him openly on the scene as the innocent son of the murdered man—and one who's going to be rich more likely than not—and in that way he meets the girl, as everyone supposes, for the first time?"

Inspector Combridge had the satisfaction, as he put forward this theory—which approximated the actual facts—of seeing approval in the eyes of Corder, Blakeway's managing clerk, and the one to-whom the actual drawing of the brief would be likely to fall. It gave him confidence.

It encouraged him to add that Blakeway's criticism had gone too far, also, when he said that they were without a theory of the way in which the crime had been committed. He thought it to be be-yond reasonable doubt that Emmoll had been lured on some false pretext to enter the car which Higgins had hired, and had then been driven to some lonely spot, where the murder had been committed.

To go farther than that might be no more than a doubtful guess, but was it not possible that Higgins had contrived to get himself hired to drive Emmoll to Southampton during the night?

There was no doubt that the procedure had been carefully planned, as was shown by a dozen details which he need not enu-merate, and they must remember that Emmoll and Higgins, what-ever their relationship, were strangers to each other. He was not sure that they had ever met previously.

Corder said there was certainly something in that, and Blake-way remarked that it was a pity that Inspector Combridge couldn't address the jury himself. By a natural sequence of ideas, he was led to ask: "Who do you want us to brief?"

"We've got to have a good man. Sir Henry"—Sir Henry Robson was the Assistant-Commissioner—"mentioned Denis Hartlin as probably the best choice."

"It's no use thinking of him. He wouldn't take it."

"You mean because he dined Emmoll earlier in the evening? I don't see why that should make any difference. We can begin from when the man calls at Miss Le Noir's, or even when he goes away."

"I don't mean because of that, though he might think it reason enough. But Hartlin once told me that if he accepted a brief in a murder prosecution he must be sure of three things: that the accused person was really guilty; that the proofs were legally sound; and that they were of such a nature as to satisfy an average English jury. He wouldn't see those conditions here."

"I won't start arguing that again. If you're sure he wouldn't, who do you think would?"

"Bullock would be the best choice. He doesn't mind starting a false scent, if he thinks the jury will follow. He'd probably talk about it as an American crime, and how we didn't want their methods of murder introduced here. In the end he'd stampede the jury into a verdict of guilty which even a stronger judge than we're likely to have wouldn't be able to check; and all they'd really mean would be that they don't want American criminal methods here."

Inspector Combridge didn't dispute this description of the methods of a very eminent counsel, but be felt that he had a better case than the solicitor was disposed to allow, and he wished it to be won, if at all, in a better way. And whether it were good or bad now, he meant it to be better before they went into court again. He said: "Well, you needn't deliver the brief for a few days yet. I must see what can be done."

He got up and went.

Combridge did not go home when he left Rinder, Blakeway & Co.'s offices, though it was Saturday afternoon and he had had a busy and anxious week, for he knew that there was much to be done in a little time. His verbal struggle with the lawyers had left him more worried in mind than he had allowed to appear. Being in this mood, he thought: "I wonder what Mr. Jellipot would make of it, as it stands now?"

On the impulse of the thought, he went into a telephone booth and soon heard the solicitor's voice at the other end of the wire.

"I thought," Inspector Combridge began, "that you might be interested to know how the Emmoll case is going, as you put me on to it at the start. I suppose you haven't heard anything of the developments of the last few days?"

"I saw that you had arrested a Mr. Higgins, and that he was remanded this morning. I don't know anything beyond the *Standard* report."

"There's a good deal behind that. But I don't say it's a clear case. Will you be at liberty if I come in now, or is it an inconvenient time?"

"No. I shall be pleased to see you. How long will you be getting here?"

"About half an hour. I'm in the Strand now."

"Very well."

Inspector Combridge got into a taxi, and almost within the time he had mentioned he was at the door of Jellipot's Bromley residence.

The solicitor received him with his usual cordiality, and when he apologized for the sudden invasion, and admitted the length of the tale that he had to tell, Jellipot answered with evident sincerity: "You needn't mind about that. I regard it as a most interesting and perplexing case. If you can really afford the time—"

"Well, I think you've given it the right word. I don't mind saying that I should like your opinion on one or two points that are still puzzling us more than a bit."

Jellipot hesitated. "I don't think," he said, "it's likely that I could help you by anything I could suggest. But in this case I will confess to a little weakness of curiosity, which may arise either from the fact that it was I who discovered the murdered man, or perhaps to some features of the case which are of somewhat unusual character."

"They are that." With this beginning, Inspector Combridge described the result of following the hint which Jellipot had given him previously. He told of the document to which Miss Manly had led him, the information which had come so opportunely from his New York colleagues, his interview with Edward Higgins, and the discovery that Higgins had been absent from his hotel on the night of the murder.

When Jellipot spoke, it was to say no more than: "It is a most interesting and surprising development. It will show you how incompetent I should be for the task of criminal investigation when I tell you that it is one which I did not expect at all."

Inspector Combridge considered this, and was not sure that it was what he had wanted to hear. "You mean," he asked bluntly, "that we are barking under the wrong tree?"

Jellipot considered his reply. "No," he said with deliberation. "I didn't mean that at all. I meant what I said. It is a matter to which I have given some thought, and I confess that this is a development which I had not foreseen at all. Does Higgins strike you as a young man who would be likely to murder his father in such a—a fantastic manner?"

"No, I don't say he does. Not particularly, that is. But that was how it was done, and when we get up against a fact like that in our profession, we find it's no use to say that nobody would."

"Yes. I appreciate that. When someone's done it, it becomes absurd to say that nobody would."

"Besides that, isn't it a possible explanation that he tried to do it in such a way that suspicion wouldn't be likely to fall on him?"

Jellipot became thoughtful again. "Yes," he said, "that is quite a plausible theory. Whether it be true—or adequate— But I confess that this is an entirely unexpected development."

"But you don't say I am on the wrong track?"

"No. I don't say that. If you press me for an opinion which I don't feel anxious to give, I should say keep an open mind. But the case is too much for me."

Inspector Combridge thanked Mr. Jellipot. Feeling no happier than before, and declining his offered hospitality with a belated memory that he had promised to take his wife out for the evening, he got up to go.

# CHAPTER XIII.

IT WAS the early part of Monday afternoon before Inspector Combridge was able to feel the elation of filling another gap in the broken tale which it was his business to reconstruct. Up to that time, he had toiled hard, neglecting his Sabbath rest, and had, in his own opinion, found little of what he sought; and in that of Superintendent Davis, with whom he sat in consultation when the short hour of his lunch was done, just nothing at all.

"We've got to find where the killing took place, even if it means asking for another remand," the superintendent said, and Inspector Combridge was about to reply that he'd be glad to hear how to begin; and that, as far as he was concerned, he could think of nothing better than hauling Miss Black over the coals again, when the telephone bell sounded. He picked up the instrument to learn that Inspector Dutton, Beaconsfield, wished to speak to the officer in charge of the Emmoll case.

He laid it down a few minutes later with a new elation in his voice as he said: "There mayn't be any need to talk about remands now. Dutton's got the house where the murder occurred. It's a tumbledown place at Loudwater that's been empty for years. He's meeting me at Beaconsfield to get me over to it before dark. There's just time for the train."

Superintendent Davis said "Well, you deserve better luck than you've had so far on this case," but finished the sentence to the sound of the closing door.

\* \* \* \* \* \* \*

Bracebridge House had been empty for more than two years. At one time it had been a manor house of some dignity, set in well-wooded grounds of five or six acres, and, had it been in good condition, might have found a purchaser at an earlier date. But it was dilapidated in ways which paint and plaster might have concealed, but which now gave it an air of dejection and exposed its years. It was like an elderly woman unkindly revealed before her morning toilet is done.

Besides this, the surrounding trees had grown too close and too large. They shut out the light. On these winter days, even at noon, the lower rooms had an air of depression which, before sunset came, would deepen to shadowy gloom.

The owner was willing to let or sell, but he would spend nothing on a property in which he had lost confidence; and on such terms it was difficult even to lease it to a responsible tenant. Augustus Grice, the Beaconsfield estate agent who had it on his books, regarded it as a waste of time to drive prospective tenants over to inspect it. When a gentleman had called upon him this Monday morning to inquire whether he had any country properties in the district for disposal at a moderate price, it was more than three months since he had had occasion to take the keys of Bracebridge House down from the keyboard on which they hung.

Even now, although his client was not discouraged by the lukewarm description he gave, he had turned his car in that direction rather from a sense of duty to the owner than in any expectation that a sale would result. When he had led the way up the neglected drive, rain-draggled and overgrown, he had intended no more than a cursory glance at the interior, unless encouraged by an enthusiasm he did not expect to rouse.

With this feeling in his mind, he had walked somewhat ahead when his client paused to observe an effect of prolonged damp on the hall ceiling. He had opened the drawing-room door, drawn back in involuntary repulsion from a stale smell of blood which lingered in the unventilated room, stared for a puzzled instant, and then taken a key from the inside of the door and locked it on the outside.

He returned to his client to lead him abruptly to the second floor, hurry him over it in a cursory manner, remark on the swift passage of time, and so conduct him back, as promptly as possible, to the waiting car.

His first impulse had been to return alone to the house and make a more private inspection. He was not unfamiliar with the unauthorized and sometimes nefarious uses which are made of unoccupied premises, and he knew that it is to the advantage of the agent responsible to deal with such events with as much reticence as the occasion allows.

But as he thought over what he had smelled and seen, the recent Jordans murder came to his mind As soon as he had got the client off his hands, he drove round to the Beaconsfield police station, and finding Inspector Dutton in, he invited him to accompany him to Bracebridge House.

Inspector Dutton said he would come at once. He went, smelled, saw, endorsed Mr. Grice's conclusion, and praised his discretion, took the keys of the house into his own custody, stationed a constable outside, and telephoned Scotland Yard, all within little more than an hour of the time when the estate agent walked into his office. It was obviously a matter for the C.I.D., but that was no reason there should be inferior efficiency on the part of the local police.

Now, with an air of brisk satisfaction, he led Inspector Combridge past the solitary constable at the door, and through a hall which would soon have succumbed to the premature twilight of the shadowing trees had he not put his hand on the switch and produced a sudden, unexpected illumination.

"Light not been cut off?" the inspector asked, in some natural surprise.

"I had it reconnected this afternoon," was the complacent answer. "I thought it would be needed by us when you would arrive." Inspector Combridge observed, as he had done before, that the local police officer was efficient in what he did.

"I haven't had anything touched," Inspector Dutton went on. "I don't even know whether the gun's loaded. I thought you'd like everything left just as it was."

He opened the drawing room door as he spoke. As he touched the switch Inspector Combridge saw, in one swift glance, the wide dark patch that spread over the oak blocks of the polished floor, the splashes on the farther wall, the length of rope, one end of which was still tied to the bars of the heavy old-fashioned grate, the automatic and the fountain-pen that lay neatly side by side on the white marble mantle-shelf.

He took three paces inwards and stood silent, striving to recreate the tragedy that the room had seen. He advanced to lean over the rope, considering its length, the strength of the bars to which it was still attached, and the twisting of the other end that still gave some indication of the way in which it had been tied round the leg of the murdered man.

Handling it as though it were hot to touch, he lifted the gun in a gloved hand.

"Loaded," he said, "fully loaded. It must have been used to frighten only, if at all. I wonder whether it belonged to Higgins or Emmoll. Well, I suppose we shall be able to find that out! And the same with the pen. If it's filled with the ink that was used for writing on the hotel bill, it ought to get us quite a long way ahead."

He felt he had come to that which might probably supply the final evidence he required. At the least, the case would not have to be taken into court with the damaging vagueness of being unable even to suggest where the murder had been committed. At the most, he might be enabled to reconstruct triumphantly what had appeared to be one of the most baffling, as it was certainly one of the most bizarre crimes, perpetrated in England in recent years.

"It looks," Inspector Dutton commented, "as though the scoundrel didn't mind the place being identified."

"So it does. It looks as though he didn't care either way. If he hadn't left these things, it might have been much harder to say that it was Emmoll who was killed here, though, if it proves to be human blood, as there's no doubt it will, it would have been a safe guess. But with these things here, which we shall almost certainly be able to identify, even apart from fingerprints for which it's too much to hope after the disappointments we've had—but on the other hand, he couldn't tell how soon they'd be discovered. They might have been found next morning, or lain unsuspected for months. It's just treating us with contempt, and he won't be the first murderer who's done that, and found his mistake too late."

The thought was not one which should have diminished his satisfaction in what he saw. It is a familiar fact that many homicidal criminals have been betrayed by their own vanity, when a meeker course of conduct would have enabled them to escape the outstretched nets of the law. Yet an uncomfortable doubt did intrude, to reduce the assurance with which he spoke. He remembered how often during this investigation he had felt the satisfaction of being "a day's march nearer home." And always to wake to the realization that he was not quite there! It was like a process of mountain climbing when each ridge gained brought a higher summit to view. What disconcerting surprise, what ingenuity of unexpected defense, might not Higgins have in the depths of his audacious and lawless mind?

# CHAPTER XIV.

THE FOLLOWING day was one of much activity, but with results which were mainly negative.

The one positive fact which was ascertained was that the fountain pen was similar to one that Tucker Emmoll had been seen to use. The ink which it contained was manufactured in the United States and corresponded both with a half-empty bottle found in the dead man's baggage and that which had been used for writing on the back of the hotel bill.

With this discovery, the authenticity of the document became reasonably certain, however puzzling its wording might be.

The automatic had not yet been definitely identified, and the fact that it was of American manufacture was inconclusive in view of the fact that both the murdered man and the accused were of that nationality. But this was a matter that the New York police had in hand, and on which they did, in fact, report definitely later in the week, establishing that it had been sold to Tucker Emmoll about eighteen months earlier.

The search for fingerprints had been vain. A few which were collected from various parts of the premises proved to be those of Mr. Grice and of persons unknown, presumably those whom he had shown, at various times, over the property. The mantelshelf bore evidence of having been wiped over.

It was clear that, however audacious the murderer's methods might appear, there were directions in which he had been most cautious in what he did.

The house bore no signs of having been broken into by violence, and as Mr. Grice was sure that all doors and windows had been left securely closed after his previous visit, and that he had found them so on this occasion, it appeared evident that the murderer must have secured duplicate keys. But this line of inquiry was blocked by the fact that the estate agent had not shown anyone over, and, as far as he was aware, the keys had not left his premises since a date prior to those on which Tucker Emmoll and Edward Higgins had landed in England.

An exhaustive inspection of the grounds had revealed nothing more than a tire-mark a few inches long which had been preserved by an overhanging laurel, at a point where a car had evidently backed in turning at the head of the drive. But this proved to be of no value when it was found that it had not been made by the car which Edward Higgins had hired, and which presumably had been used to convey the victim to the scene of his violent death.

In the midst of the energetic pursuit of these investigations, Inspector Combridge found time to call upon Miss Manly, and met with a firm though polite rebuff.

"My niece," she says, "knows nothing whatever about Mr. Emmoll's death, and, her age being what it is, and under the circumstances of the case, I have advised her that there is no occasion to discuss the matter with you at all. She particularly wished me to tell you, however, that she is convinced that Edward Higgins had nothing to do with the matter."

"Do you," he asked shrewdly, having some confidence both in Miss Manly's intelligence and in her veracity, and much less in her entire ignorance as to how that incriminating document came to be planted upon her, "give that as your own opinion, or only as a message from her?"

Miss Manly considered this, showing no desire either to evade the question, or any haste to reply. If Prudence had worded her message in a slightly less emphatic manner! But "nothing to do with the matter?" That was to say much. And the last confidence she had from the girl had been of a dubious kind, leaving the character of Edward Higgins in doubt on more points than this. She also thought, as Inspector Combridge had done, of the puzzle of the appearance of that document in her own wood, as she answered, "Do you think that is quite a fair question, Inspector? I don't see why I should have an opinion on the matter worth giving you. My niece has known the young man much longer than I—in fact, I don't know him at all.

"It is a message from her. But I will add that I am sure it expresses her sincere conviction, and it might be wise for you to attach some weight to it for that reason."

"She doesn't deny that she is engaged to Higgins?"

"She neither denies nor asserts anything on the subject. I don't see it to be a question that concerns you in any way. It isn't an offense in English law, as far as I am aware, to be acquainted with a young man who may afterwards be accused of a crime of which he may be quite innocent."

"I didn't say that it is. But when a crime of this nature has been committed, it is the duty of every citizen to render all the help she or he can, so that justice may be done, even though it may be a very unpleasant matter for them."

"I don't know," Miss Manly replied, being quite willing to lead the conversation away to abstract discussion, at which she felt quite able to hold her own, "that the question arises in any form, as I have told you already that my niece denies any knowledge of the matter. But when you talk of justice, may you not be using the wrong word? How can any justice be done when a man is dead? You can do no justice to him.

"Would not retribution be a more accurate word? Are we not all morally required, individually as well as nationally, to observe justice, in the sense that we must not be less than just to our fellow men, but in no sense beyond that, or any act of mercy or forgiveness would be a sin?"

"Well," the inspector replied, exasperated, "if you mean we ought to let men cut each other up, and tell them the State forgives them for what they do!"

"I don't think I said anything that implied that," Miss Manly replied, with a smile that made amity of her words, "whatever my beliefs on that subject may happen to be. What I suggested was that

justice, in the sense in which you used the word, is not a moral obligation at all, even if it be consistent with the Christianity which
most of us profess; and that retribution would be a little more accurate."

"Well, I won't argue that," Inspector Combridge replied good-
humouredly, though continuing to press his point with characteristic
persistence. "But if the young lady's so sure that Higgins hasn't
done anything wrong, wouldn't it be more natural for her to say so
herself, and tell me anything she can to support her opinion? We're
bound to think, if she keeps away from us like this, that there isn't
much good she's got to say."

Miss Manly again considered this without instant reply. "Of
course," she said finally, as though choosing her words with care,
"you may draw such a conclusion, but it doesn't sound reasonable to
me. If she knows—I don't say she does or doesn't—anything in favour of Mr. Higgins, wouldn't it be more in order for her to communicate it to his own solicitors?"

"No. I don't see that it would. We only want to be fair. She
can't do better than tell us, if she knows anything that tends to show
he's an innocent man. But if she knows anything up the opposite
street, and she's still as fond of him as ever, it would explain why
she's trying to keep away."

"I've told you already, Inspector," Miss Manly replied, "that
she says she knows nothing about the murder—nothing whatever."

"Well, I'm sorry," Inspector Combridge retorted with a firmness rather more evident, and a courtesy that seemed to maintain
itself with greater difficulty, "but while I haven't seen the young
lady, and she won't speak for herself, I must keep an open mind
about that."

It was early next morning that he saw Superintendent Davis to
report the progress he had made, and to learn of any other developments which had occurred.

There was one minor detail—one of those scraps of doubtful
testimony which may be all or nothing in the final count—which
had been obtained by one of his colleagues who had been engaged
in questioning the staff of Willing's Hotel.

The waiter there said that Mr. Higgins was fond of fruit. He would frequently eat a raw apple at the end of a meal, and in doing this it had been his habit to use a small clasp-knife from his own pocket rather than to utilize the table cutlery. At least, it had been until after one of his longer absences, when he had remarked, with an air of vexation, that he must have mislaid the knife, and the waiter had not seen it again.

Was it a pearl-handled knife? It was white. The waiter would not go beyond that. He seemed to be in an honest doubt.

Could he not say definitely that it was after the weekend of the murder that it had been missing? Again he hesitated. He was not sure. He was more inclined to think that it was at an earlier date—say after Mr. Higgins was understood to have returned from Glasgow. But he could not go beyond that. He had attached no importance to it at the time, and he was not sure.

This was, at least, honest evidence, such as will sometimes be more potent to sway a jury than a glib tongue that remembers all the prosecution requires.

"I don't think much of it myself," the superintendent said frankly "but Corder says we should put the waiter on the stand. He said it may do a bit of good, and can do no harm. By the way, when I had Corder on the phone about this, he mentioned that Hartlin won't take the brief."

"Blakeway said he wouldn't yesterday. I wonder they asked him at all. What reason did he give?"

"He said he had too much on hand for the next six weeks already."

"Did he know that we've found where Emmoll was killed?"

"No, I don't see how he could. Corder hadn't heard of it when he sounded him."

"Well, Blakeway wants Bullock. He ought to be good enough."

"Not if Hartlin's against us."

"But why should he be that? If he's too busy?"

"The *Sunday Mail* has instructed Jellipot to act for Higgins. You know he's friendly with Hartlin. He's almost sure to try for him, and he'll get him if anyone can." Inspector Combridge frowned over this information. His experiences had been more fortunate when Mr. Jellipot had been acting with him than when they had been on opposite sides. The combination of Hartlin instructed by Jellipot was not one of which he cared to think. Not in a case as ragged as this still was. He said. "Jellipot never moves quickly, unless he's obliged. He won't have approached Hartlin yet. Why shouldn't I see him now?"

"Why should you?"

"I should feel easier if he took the brief."

"How do you think you can manage that?"

"Tell him what more we've found out. He'll see it's a better case than he thought. Hartlin likes to win, as they all do."

"It's a bit out of routine. But I don't see why you shouldn't try. Especially as you've seen him about the case already.

"You can tell him we've no doubt that we've got the right man, but it's a difficult case, and that Sir Henry—or you can say Mr. Lansford himself—says the Home Secretary is particularly anxious that he shouldn't refuse the brief."

Inspector Combridge had thought his day was done, but he saw that this was not a matter to leave till the next morning. He went at once, and his promptness was rewarded by finding the barrister in his chambers, as he had been on the occasion of the previous interview.

Mr. Hartlin received his visitor affably, but said at once that his decision was final. "I've told you before that I don't think Emmoll was any loss, and I may add that I don't like your case. It's strong on some points, but on others it's weak. If I took the brief, I mightn't feel able to press for a conviction quite as hard as you'd think I ought. While I feel like that, to take it wouldn't be fair to myself or you."

"But it may be a stronger case than you suspect. We've found out a lot more during the last twenty-four hours."

"Well, I'm willing to listen."

"We've found where the murder took place, and among other things, the actual pen with which the confession—if that's the right name for it—was written. It's a place called Bracebridge House—"

"Bracebridge House? I think I know where that is. Isn't it at Loudwater? A fine old place, but rather fallen into decay?"

"Yes. That's the place."

"I went over it with my wife—Grice, the estate agent at Beacons field put us onto it—about four months ago. I've been looking for something of the kind to buy for some time past, but I've been too busy to settle on anything.

"I remember the place because I felt tempted to make an offer—I believe it can be bought for almost nothing—but my wife took a dislike to it. She thought it depressing, and didn't seem able to visualize what it might become if it were renovated and the trees pruned back from the windows. I recall her saying that it was the sort of place where a murder might have occurred. I wonder what she'd say now if I'd bought it!"

"Well," Inspector Combridge replied, having a practical mind, "if you'd bought it then I don't suppose there'd have been one there at all."

"No. I suppose not. If I'd bought it, Emmoll might not have died, or died in a different way. Consequences are queer things. But you'd better not develop that idea further, or you'll be making Mrs. Hartlin an accessory before the fact. What have you found out there?"

Inspector Combridge described what he had found, and became conscious, as the barrister listened in an attentive silence, of how far he still was from having solved the problem with which he dealt. But when Mr. Hartlin spoke at last, it was to congratulate rather than to point out the difficulties that still remained.

"You have certainly," he said, "made a most important advance, and I needn't tell you that it's patience—and persistence—that win at last. If I should ever commit a murder—and it's a crime that's possible to almost all of us under sufficient provocation—I don't know that there's any officer in the C.I.D. that I wouldn't rather have hunting me down.

"And as to those tire marks not agreeing, I shouldn't attach much importance to that. Under evergreen shelter, as you say they are, they may have lasted for months. In fact, I wouldn't mind making an even bet that it's from the wheel of my own car.

"From what you say, I should think we were about the last people who used that drive—that's excepting Mr. Emmoll's little party, of course—and I remember that Blake had some difficulty in turning. You may have observed that I have rather a large car. But as to taking the brief—I wasn't merely refusing in a polite manner when I said I'm overloaded with work already. And I don't like the case, even as it stands now. I don't like it on principle, whether you've arrested the right man or not. But I won't give you an offhand reply. I'll think it over, and send you a written answer tomorrow."

Inspector Combridge rose reluctantly. He felt that he had failed, and yet there was little more to be said.

"At least," he asked, "if you decide you can't take it, we shan't find that you're on the other side?"

"No. I don't think you will. As a matter of fact, I haven't been asked. But, of course, when I say that, it's not a promise. It's mere anticipation of probability."

The next morning brought the barren result of this interview in a letter from which Superintendent Davis read out an abstract from which neither he nor Inspector Combridge derived any satisfaction. Hartlin had written:

> *The case, as it now stands, if I have appreciated it accurately, falls definitely short of the proof which the law requires. In taking it into court, it would be necessary to rely almost entirely upon the effect which would be produced on the minds of the jury if Higgins should refuse to go on the witness stand to give an account of his reasons for hiring the car, and of his movements on the night of the crime; or should he attempt to give such an explanation, and fail to do so convincingly.*
>
> *In other words, the prosecution would rely upon the inability of the accused to prove his innocence. Although this is a procedure which is becoming established by custom, especially in prosecutions of this*

*character, since accused persons have been permitted to give evidence in their own defense, it is not one to which I have ever been a consenting party. I hold that it transgresses a fundamental and valuable principle of English law.*

# CHAPTER XV.

MR. JELLIPOT greeted the lady, whom he now met for the first time, with a diffident friendliness which would have put a more nervous woman than Miss Manly at ease. In her case, it raised a doubt as to the sufficiency of this quiet and elderly Solicitor for the task which had been laid upon him. But the thought did not linger, for the defense of Edward Higgins was not a matter with which she was greatly concerned, and there was a directness in Jellipot's words, if not in his manner, which quickly concentrated her mind upon the purpose for which she came.

"I am pleased to see you, Miss Manly," he said, "but it is your niece whom I am particularly anxious to meet."

"I am not sure that would be wise. And it is a course to which her parents are very much opposed."

"In her interests may I ask, or in those of my client?"

"In her interests, naturally, I can't say that they are greatly concerned for Mr. Higgins, so long as her name can be saved from any association with him."

"In that case, may I conclude that, from their point of view, his acquittal might produce the more difficult situation for them?"

Miss Manly hesitated. "I should not like to imply—it would be unjust—that they desire him to be condemned, and especially not so if he should be an innocent man. But it is no doubt true that if he were found to be guilty they would be relieved from a position which they intensely dislike."

"From which I must conclude that Miss Prudence's feelings haven't changed?"

"No. She is resolved to marry him if and when it may be possible."

"And she believes in his innocence?"

"Yes. Absolutely."

"Yet she will not see me, to give me any help in her power?"

"At present she'll only do so if Mr. Higgins himself should ask her."

"So I am to conclude that there is nothing helpful she would be able to say?"

"No. Not necessarily."

"Or even that she may know something which would be detrimental to his defense?" he queried ironically.

"I feel that would be a mistaken conclusion."

"But are you sure you know everything—that she has been frank with you without reserve?"

"I feel confident that she has."

"Perhaps more so than with her parents?"

"She hasn't seen her parents at all. She is still with me."

"Which does not answer my question."

"Perhaps not. What she told me was confidential. I've conveyed it to her parents so far as I've had her permission to do so."

Jellipot saw that, if he had not been answered before, he was answered now. It was clear that the girl had confided matters to her aunt which she was less willing either that her parents should know or that she should disclose to him. It was clear also that Miss Manly, in whose discretion he felt some confidence, and who was in evident sympathy with her niece, was disposed to support this attitude.

Possibly it might be wise. It might be a confidence which would embarrass him in his client's defense. But, all the same, he preferred to know. He was the one to judge. He went on less with a direct object in what he said than with the thought that, if he were to learn more, the conversation must be sustained.

"Her parents are rather difficult?"

"It would be scarcely fair to say that. The situation is one that most people would dislike. My brother, by the standards that I should apply, is a particularly broadminded man."

"But he would have opposed such an engagement under almost any circumstances?"

"Yes. I think he would."

"And Mrs. Manly?"

"Mrs. Manly, at times, can be a little difficult."

Mr. Jellipot considered the implication of this admission, but when he spoke again, it was to revert to the original subject.

"You will, I am sure, appreciate," he said, "that the defense of Mr. Higgins presents, under the most favourable circumstances, some features of particular difficulty. These are greatly increased if I cannot feel that I have received his full confidence, and that of those who are friendly to him."

"Do you mean that, as matters now stand, he is in serious danger of being convicted of the murder of Tucker Emmoll? I should be glad if you would give me a frank reply, for I am reminded that I promised to ask you that."

"Am I to understand that Miss Prudence's attitude may be influenced by my reply?"

"I don't think she would readily believe that he is in any real peril of conviction on such a charge."

"But if she were?"

"I cannot say."

"But you know what you would advise her to do?"

"I'm not even sure about that."

"My opinion is that in the absence of any further evidence being obtained against him, Edward Higgins has little to fear, if he can give a completely satisfactory account of how he was occupied during the night of the murder, and the three following days. If he cannot do that, he is in real peril of a conviction against which an appeal could be made, but might not succeed."

"I'm sorry to hear that you regard the position so seriously."

"Am I to conclude from that, Miss Manly, that you think he will be unable to give a satisfactory account of his movements on the dates in question?"

"No. Please don't. That is a question for him to answer."

"And I think you said that your niece will be prepared to give any evidence in her power if Higgins should ask her to do so?"

"Yes. She asked me to say that. But I don't think he will."

"Neither do I. At the interview which I had with him last night, his principal anxiety appeared to be that she should not be drawn into the matter in any way. But whether this was out of consideration for himself or her, you may be able to judge better than I."

"Yes," Miss Manly assented, "perhaps I can." But she did not offer to explain what her judgment was. She said: "Thank you. I'll talk it over with Prudence again," and got up to go.

# CHAPTER XVI.

IT WAS during the latter part of the following morning that Jellipot returned to his office, after a long interview with the accused man. He had been unable to shake Higgins' resolution that the girl to whom he was engaged should not go on the witness-stand in his behalf. When he entered the office he was informed that Miss Prudence Manly had called, and requested an interview. "Show her in," he said, and looked up a moment later to greet a younger visitor than he had expected to see.

"My aunt has told me," she began, even as Jellipot was guiding her to the client's chair, "what you said yesterday, and I decided to come and explain everything."

The voice was timid and low, and it was easy to see that she was nervous. But there was a directness in the substance of what she said, which reminded him of his visitor of the previous day. She had more beauty, even apart from her fresher youth, than could be credited to the older woman, but there was yet an evident likeness, as though the elder Prudence Manly had been cast again in a softer and smaller mold. This girl might not be able to face the problems of life with Miss Manly's cheerful, humorous smile, but, with sufficient cause, she might be equally tenacious, equally stubborn to take her own road to her chosen goal.

"It was," Mr. Jellipot replied, with a kindly gravity, "a wise, and perhaps I may add, a brave decision."

He was conscious, as he said this, of a sudden glance from the long-lashed eyes. He knew their question to be: "Why do you say that? Why do you call it brave? How much do you guess or know?"

He was quick to add: "I have had a talk with Mr. Higgins since your aunt was here yesterday. You may like to know that he has now given me a full account of certain matters which he had previously withheld. So far as I can judge, there may be nothing for you to tell."

"He told you *everything*?"

"So I suppose."

"And he will let me—"

"No. He will not hear of your going on the witness-stand under any circumstances."

"And if I don't, he will be tried for this horrid thing?"

"Yes. I think we must anticipate that."

"But you can call me without his consent?"

"I'm afraid not."

"But how could he stop that? What could he do?"

"Probably nothing. But it would be an act of professional misconduct which would be—I will not say impossible; few things are—but it would approach impossibility in the mind of any responsible solicitor. I should deserve to be struck off the rolls for conniving such an act."

"But you could—you could refuse to defend him unless he agrees? You could persuade—you could make him see!"

"No. I don't think I could. But I must tell you frankly, Miss Prudence, that it is a decision with which I agree."

The girl said "Oh!" to this in a startled, astonished way. "Then I needn't have come? You can do it another way?" And the relief in her voice showed how great had been her dread of that which she had offered to do.

To her second question, Mr. Jellipot avoided direct reply. He said: "I'm very glad you are here. And, if I may, I'll ask you two questions, which you need not answer; but if you are able to do so in the way I hope, it will be a pleasure to hear."

"Yes. I'll answer anything. I came here to do that."

"Very well. Do you know anything whatever concerning the death of Tucker Emmoll, beyond what has appeared in the newspapers?"

"No. Nothing at all." She said this with a note of relief in her voice, as though the question had been unexpectedly easy, and he wondered whether she would be able to deal with the next in the same manner.

"I am glad to hear it," he said, "though not surprised. Do you know anything whatever concerning the document which was found in your aunt's grounds, either concerning how it was written, or how it came to be there?"

"No. How should I? Nothing at all."

"So I supposed. But I am glad to have it from your own lips."

It was only a few minutes after Prudence had left Mr. Jellipot's office, and he was still sitting back in apparent idleness while he considered what a good jury-conquering witness she would have been likely to make, when he was called by the editor of the *Sunday Mail*, who inquired what counsel he was intending to brief.

"I can't say," Mr. Jellipot answered, "that I have decided at present. I have discussed the question with Mr. Higgins, who says, naturally enough, that he doesn't know enough about our barristers to have any opinion worth giving, and he leaves it to me entirely."

"Yes, of course. What I asked was who you'd like to have. We don't restrict you. It's public knowledge now that we are financing Higgins' defense, and we want it properly done."

"There are some advantages in not briefing counsel until after the preliminary hearing. In the event of a committal, which I am disposed to think that it may be difficult to avoid—"

"Of course there'll be a committal! I wasn't questioning that. What I want to know is who you propose to brief."

Jellipot controlled a mild irritation which was roused both by the manner and substance of this reply. He saw that the *Sunday Mail* assumed that his client would be committed for trial, and probably that he would be convicted and hanged. But they wished the event to be staged in a spectacular manner, suitable to their own dignity, without anticipating or caring that it would make any difference to the result.

But he could not undertake such a defense without exhausting every possibility that it allowed, and he knew that there are few "of courses" in the process of English law.

"What I have been considering," he went on, "is whether it will not be best in my client's interests that I should represent him in the magistrate's court, and defer—"

The editor broke in abruptly. There was often a delusive diffidence in Mr. Jellipot's voice when he was most obstinate in his mood, and this was accentuated now by a general reluctance to assert his own judgment on so personal an issue, or to seem to attribute ability to himself superior to that of the practiced advocates of the bar. The hesitant, deprecating tone may have had its influence in suggesting Mr. Jellipot's unsuitability for the part he was so unexpectedly proposing, and it may have been a real consideration for the prisoner's interests, as well as for the prestige of the paper he edited, that edged the editor's impatient words. He exclaimed: "But that won't do, Mr. Jellipot. It really won't. Not in a case like this. We've just heard that the prosecution are briefing Bullock, and Ritchie, and Gayland-Jones. You can't expect to stand up to all them. It isn't fair to Higgins, and it wouldn't do us any good."

"I hadn't heard," Jellipot replied, "that they'd got Gayland-Jones. I should have thought that Bullock and Ritchie would have been enough, especially as Bullock always goes his own way. It doesn't look as though they're over-happy about their case. There's a proverb about having too many cooks. But I quite see your point. I'll talk it over with Higgins again. Who would you like to have?"

"We should prefer Hartlin, of course. He'll stand up to Bullock, as there aren't many who will. I hear that he refused the brief for the Crown."

"Then he's not likely to take ours."

"Well, you can try. If you can get him, you needn't haggle about the fee."

It may be doubted whether Jellipot had altered either his opinion or his intention, but he answered deliberately: "I'll see him this afternoon and do what I can to persuade him to take it." And he was not likely on such a matter to promise that which he did not mean.

"Thank you, Mr. Jellipot. I felt sure you'd see it in the right light Of course you'll understand that there is no reflection upon your own abilities. We have great confidence in you. But in a position like this—"

"I have had little experience in criminal advocacy," Jellipot replied seriously, "and I should accept it as a reasonable deduction that my ability may be equally lacking."

He laid down the telephone, and sat for a time in thoughtful silence. "Well," he said half-aloud at last, "perhaps it may be the best way." He reached for the instrument again, and said he wished to be put through to Mr. Hartlin's offices.

It was during the following afternoon that the editor of the *Sunday Mail* telephoned again to inquire the result of Jellipot's efforts.

"I am sorry," the solicitor answered, with a note of nervousness in his voice which went beyond his customary diffidence of tone or manner, "but I was not successful in persuading Hartlin to accept the brief. I may say that I did all I could, but I am afraid his refusal is final."

The editor thought Jellipot's tone was more serious than the occasion required. He would have liked Hartlin to appear, but, if he wouldn't, it was not a matter about which anyone need lose sleep, unless it were Higgins himself.

"That's a pity," he answered cheerfully; "but if he won't there's no more to be said. After all, when he'd refused the other side, it wasn't likely he would. Have you anyone else in mind?"

"I don't propose to brief anyone for the moment, in view of Hartlin's attitude. I had another conference with my client this morning, and his instructions are now definite that I shall represent him on Monday."

"But I told you yesterday, Mr. Jellipot, that we are not satisfied with that procedure. I can understand that it would be a valuable advertisement for you, but there are other considerations. I don't want to be rude, but, frankly, if you persist in that attitude, we'll have to consider placing the case in other hands "

Mr. Jellipot was a worried man. He had made, as he said, a most earnest effort to induce Denis Hartlin to accept the brief. A long conference at the barrister's office had been followed by an adjournment to the Savoy, at which Mr. Hartlin had not guided him to the corner table where he was accustomed to dine, and where he had, in fact, entertained Emmoll. But on this occasion, he had ordered a private room, and it had been after ten-thirty when Mr. Jellipot had departed at last, with the realization that he had failed.

After that, Mr. Jellipot had had a bad night, and a long conference with his client, which had occupied most of the morning, had not improved his spirits or lightened the cloud of anxiety which had fallen upon him.

He had anticipated some difficulty—even some unpleasantness—with the editor of the *Sunday Mail*, and was fair enough to observe that the man had some reason to be annoyed, for it is a matter of proverbial equity he who pays the piper should call the tune. He was prepared to be apologetic, though he had no intention of giving way. But the suggestion that he could be actuated by a desire for self-advertisement in reaching such a decision had the rousing effect of a sudden blow, and it was in a very different tone from that which he had formerly used that he replied: "I am afraid you misconceive the position. I take instructions from my client, and from him alone. Whether he proposes to change his solicitor is for him to decide."

The editor of the *Sunday Mail* was not usually short of words, but for a moment speech failed. Then he asked: "If we decide to withdraw our support unless he changes his solicitor, where will he be then?"

"He will be represented by my office, as he is now."

Saying this on an impulse of anger which may have had no precedent in the whole of his professional career, Jellipot hung up the receiver.

He regretted this at the next moment, and doubly so when he found that the editor made no effort to re-establish connection with him, for he observed the probability that the *Sunday Mail* would make an immediate effort to persuade Edward Higgins to change his solicitor, and he had become particularly anxious to retain and handle the case in his own way But the only sequel was a letter which reached him by hand a couple of hours later from the newspaper's legal department, and this said no more than that the editor regretted his decision, and wished to put on record that he had been prepared to provide adequate counsel for the prisoner's defense.

For the fact was that the editor had referred the matter, in his first moment of indignation, to the tame barrister who, as is the Fleet Street custom, was usually on the premises for consultation in such emergencies, and had been informed that Mr. Jellipot was, unfortunately, right; and that, apart from the consent of Edward Higgins, they could do nothing at all. Indeed, it was legally doubtful whether they could withdraw their undertaking to finance the defense, even though Higgins might prefer legal aid which they did not approve. And, in short, they would do well to accept with dignity what they could not change, and especially as Mr. Jellipot had the reputation of having reason for what he did.

But this letter brought little peace to the solicitor's troubled mind. "I resented it," he thought, "when it was suggested that I could put self-interest before that of my client. And it was natural to do so, for the charge was false. But would it have been more unprofessional—would it have been worse—than that which I am planning now?"

\* \* \* \* \* \* \*

Mr. Jellipot had had an anxious weekend, but he had come at last to the peace of those who have settled minds, and on Sunday night he slept well. As he looked round the small, overcrowded court, he seemed placid enough. Indeed, it might be thought that he was too unconcerned, too oblivious of the strength of legal talent arrayed against him, perhaps too dull even to be aware of his own inadequacy for the battle he had to do.

He had reached over the dock-rail to shake hands with the prisoner, whom he had not seen since Friday, but had said no more than a cheerful greeting to a man who looked self-possessed enough, though his face showed some signs of the solitary ordeal of the past week. But Jellipot had remarked on Friday that there would be no gain in further meetings, unless there should be something new to discuss, and—well, the waiting was over now!

Mr. Jellipot, looking round the court, saw some faces he knew, but most of those who had been chorus to the tragedy, before or after, were not there. One by one, they would be brought into the court from the witness' room, and would add their item of testimony, would weave their strand in the net that was to enmesh Edward Higgins at last, unless he should be equal to tear it through. Miss Manly was not there. They were calling her. But he saw and smiled at the younger Prudence, who smiled back in a pale way.

A tall, grave man sat at her side, with enough likeness to Miss Manly to make it an easy guess that the girl's father, though he might not approve, would not desert his daughter when he had learned that she would not change her purpose to come. Now he was looking at Edward Higgins with an intent gaze, as though he would penetrate, by sheer force of will, the question of the guilt or innocence of this young alien who had shaken the peace of his well-ordered, God-fearing home. While he looked at the prisoner, his hand held that of his daughter in a firm grip. Evidently, division of judgment had not led to loss of sympathy between the two. Jellipot was pleased to observe that, because he designed an unexpected trouble for the younger Prudence before the case in that court should close.

He was recalled from his thoughts by realization that the magistrates' clerk was leaning over to speak to him.

"I understand," he said, "that the prosecution will not ask for a further adjournment. They tell me that they think today and tomorrow should be enough to enable them to finish. If you are proposing to reserve your defense, or would be unlikely to require more than the following day, we could arrange to go straight ahead, and get the committal in time for it to be set down for the next sessions. But, of course, if you feel you will need more time—"

It was no more than an inquiry of routine, based on the necessity of prearranging the work of the court, and influenced by the curious legal fiction that murderers are always anxious to be tried as promptly as possible, but Jellipot felt bound to object to an implication that it contained.

"I certainly do not intend," he answered, with more firmness in the words than in the way in which they were spoken, "to reserve the defense. I intend to oppose a committal. I shall ask the court to dismiss the charge."

The magistrates' clerk looked at the ranked array of Mr. Jellipot's legal adversaries, now busily whispering and apparently joking among themselves: Mr. Bullock, K.C., Mr. Ritchie, Mr. Gayland-Jones. And seated before them, Mr. Blakeway and Mr. Corder and Mr. Corder's clerk. And with the prestige, the authority of the Home Office in what they did. And Mr. Jellipot said mildly that he would oppose these gentlemen in their legal procession to the higher court! But he gave no sign of his thoughts, as he asked courteously: "Do you have many witnesses to call? Do you think Wednesday will be enough?"

Jellipot replied that he had not yet decided what evidence he would call, but he did not think it would be necessary for him to occupy the court for more than a few hours at the most. He thought Wednesday would be enough.

\* \* \* \* \* \* \*

Mr. Bullock stated his case at some length, though to accuse him of prolixity might be unjust. He gave points to items of evidence which were to come, some of which, apart from his adroit inferences and implications, might have been less easy to see.

But he did not labour these, for the time (as he supposed) of actual battle was far ahead. The defense surely admitted that, when they put up no gladiator of his own weight to contest his words. All he had to do now was to make a demonstration of strength. To parade his witnesses before the court to an extent sufficient to win permission to put Edward Higgins in peril of death by a jury's vote.

As he spoke, the reporters' pencils moved rapidly, for the tale he told was of what they called a "sensational" kind, and much of it had not been made public before.

Yet he was scrupulous not to assert more, except as matter of legitimate argument, than he would have evidence to support. He lost nothing by that. He could bring it in with more dramatic effect when he came to the document so strangely found in Miss Manly's wood.

So he began with Tucker Emmoll's visit to England, a wealthy, leisured, American citizen, coming over to visit the land of his birth and his early years. He passed on at once to the night of the tragedy—Friday, January 20$^{th}$. They would hear that he had booked his passage from Southampton, from which place he would have sailed on the following day. They would hear from the hotel-porter that he sent on his luggage, he paid his bill—a document destined to reappear under very singular circumstances—he called for a taxi at an early hour of the evening, and left the hotel. Bullock paused for effect and continued.

After that it appeared—though it did not seem to have any bearing upon the tragedy, in view of what was known of Emmoll's subsequent movements—but it appeared to be a fact that he dined at the Savoy with a well-known member of the English bar. From this place he proceeded to make a farewell call upon a lady—a Miss Le Noir—whose acquaintance he had made while in this country—and who would tell the court that he left her house in Marsden Terrace at or about 2:00 A.M., with the expressed intention of travelling to Southampton by car.

"From the moment that Mr. Emmoll left Miss Le Noir's house," the learned counsel continued impressively, "he was not seen alive again, nor have the most exhaustive inquiries been able to discover that he did, in fact, engage any vehicle to take him to Southampton that night. Nothing more of his movements is known until his dead body was found, stripped and exposed with the most callous indecency..."—Bullock turned a hard gaze upon the prisoner as he said this, as though expecting him to flinch visibly from this mention of the shocking manner in which the body had been displayed to the public gaze—"...upon the roadside stile of the peaceful village of Jordans—the quiet historic Quaker village that—"

At this point Bullock met the glance of the presiding magistrate, and reminded himself that there was no jury there, and that the facts and his more or less legitimate deductions therefrom were all that the present court was interested to hear. He ended, rather weakly: "That is in the middle—more or less—of Buckinghamshire.

"Within forty-eight hours of that discovery—first made, by a singular coincidence, by my friend Mr. Jellipot, who is appearing for the prisoner—a parcel containing the clothes and some other effects of the murdered man, together with a stanza of ribald verse to which I shall revert, was found where it had evidently been deposited by the murderer on a footpath in the Chiltern Hills. And more recently, still in the same district, in an empty house at Loudwater, an estate agent, Mr. Augustus Grice, will tell the court how he came upon a blood-drenched room in which were two articles—a loaded revolver and a fountain pen—which have been identified as the property of Tucker Emmoll, and one at least of which is known to have been in his possession within a few hours of his death.

"The evidence which connects Edward Higgins with these events is entirely of a circumstantial character, but...."—here Mr. Bullock interposed the remarks usual to such occasions upon the value of that class of evidence, which may be passed over—"...in this instance this evidence is cumulative, and I may describe it as overwhelming.

"Shortly after Mr. Emmoll landed in this country, the prisoner, who is a native of the United States, also sailed from New York. On arrival in London, he put up at one of our smaller residential ho-tels—Willing's Hotel, Bloomsbury Street—where, with occasional absences, during which he retained his room, he quietly remained until about ten days ago, when, having evidently completed what-ever matter had brought him here, he booked a return passage to his native land.

"What," Mr. Bullock asked, with another lapse towards his more dramatic manner, "was that purpose, and what connection had he with the murdered man?

139

"To begin the answer to that question, we come to one of the most extraordinary incidents of this amazing crime. It is an incident—"

Here the learned counsel proceeded to describe the finding of the hotel bill with its endorsed "confession" in Miss Manly's grounds. He emphasized that it was a paper which must have been in Tucker Emmoll's pocket at the time of his death; that it was written with ink similar to that of his fountain pen, which was not easily procurable in this country; and he said that experts would be called to prove that it was in the handwriting of the murdered man.

"I suggest," he said, "that there can be no reasonable doubt that it was penned by Tucker Emmoll within a few hours of his violent death, and that the more closely it be considered the more deadly its meaning will become.

"In the first place, it is difficult to consider its wording without coming to the conclusion that, while it may be a genuine document in the sense that it is in Tucker Emmoll's handwriting, it is not genuine in the sense that it was not an act of his own volition. He did not intend or desire to take his own life, and few things can be more certain than that he did not do so. The subsequent disposal of the body, of the clothes, of this document itself, show that the agency of the tragedy remained in sinister activity after his life had closed. Permit me to elaborate on this.

"It requires no strain of imagination to conclude that the man who forced Tucker Emmoll to pen this document was the one by whose hand he died; and to whose advantage—it is natural to ask—should its existence be? To whom but to the man whom Tucker Emmoll names as his son—the man who, in the name of Edward Higgins, is before you now?

"It may or may not be necessary—it is a matter which is now under legal consideration—to go into the question of the actual relationship between these two men, or to consider the cause of enmity which existed between them. If it should be decided that it is advisable to bring witnesses from the United States to prove these antecedent circumstances, I need scarcely say that the defense will receive due notice before the trial of the accused.

"For the present, it will be sufficient to say—and I presume this will not be challenged by the defense—that it is on the records of the courts of that country that the mother of Edward Higgins had brought an unsuccessful suit against Tucker Emmoll to establish that he was the father of the prisoner, and that she has been imprisoned in that country quite recently for refusing to obey a court order that she should cease to represent herself as his lawful wife.

"If that be so, it is evident that when Edward Higgins sailed for England he had a strong reason to hate his father—if such he were—and as strong a reason, of another kind, to desire that he should not die without supplying some evidence of the marriage that Lucille Higgins claimed. It was a case where revenge and cupidity cried with the same voice, and urged him on the same way.

"For Tucker Emmoll was a wealthy man. If no will be found—and I understand that none has yet been heard of—that document must go far to establish Edward Higgins and his mother as the heirs of the murdered man."

Having sufficiently stressed the abundance of motive, Mr. Bullock went on to the question of opportunity, and laid equal stress, though perhaps not more than it fairly deserved, upon the evidence he proposed to call showing that the prisoner had absented himself from his hotel on the night of the crime, and that he had hired, from a nearby garage, a closed car which he had returned on the fourth day, without explanation of where he had been in the meantime.

Motive and opportunity! Who could reasonably doubt that it was Tucker Emmoll—Tucker Emmoll, who would be requiring a car that night, and who could not be found to have procured it from any other source—for whom Edward Higgins had hired that vehicle?

By what careful plot he had lured his victim to engage him as driver that night might never be known. But it was material to observe that, whatever their relationship, the two men might not have met, if at all, within recent years; that while Tucker Emmoll might have been utterly off his guard, not suspecting that he had a foe of any kind in this land to which he had returned from so long an absence, his pursuer had had weeks of leisure in which to observe, to plan, and to weave his net.

Motive and opportunity—they went far, but it might be said that they did not go far enough. Suspicion, however strong, was not proof. And if there were no more than that, the power of the law, however reluctantly, might have held its hand, and let the murderer go back to his native land to enjoy the fruit of this monstrously conceived crime.

But fortunately there *was* more. There was that damning document found in Miss Manly's wood. And to show how damning it was—how clearly and conclusively it identified the murderer with the man now in the dock—it was necessary to observe a separate circumstance which Edward Higgins doubtless had not expected to come to the notice of the police.

"Why—" counsel went on. "Why was that document deposited in Miss Manly's wood? The exact motive in the murderer's mind may be doubtful. Human motives are often obscure even to those to whom they belong. But one thing is certain. It was not chance. The odds against that must be many thousands to one.

"Miss Prudence Manly will be called, and she will swear that she had no previous knowledge either of the criminal, or the crime, or the murdered man. She had not previously even heard Edward Higgins' name.

"When she found this document carefully secured by its stone weights under the old umbrella, her only concern was to decide a point of conscience as to whether she should report a matter to the police which might be instrumental in bringing the extreme penalty of the law on a fellowman or whether she should keep quiet about it.

"It is a point of conscience which we can respect, though we may not share it; and Miss Manly will tell us that, when Inspector Combridge called upon her, she had already decided that it was her duty to report the incident.

"Miss Manly is a lady of good character, holding an honoured place in a community that has a deserved reputation both for the simplicity and severity of its moral code. I put her forward without hesitation as a truthful witness.

142

"But Miss Manly has a niece. A niece living at Marlow, who happens to be of the same name as herself, and it will be shown that—probably without the knowledge of her parents or other relatives—this younger lady was acquainted with the prisoner; that, since he has landed in England, they have had a regular habit of meeting twice a week at a tea room about three miles from her home. They met sometimes in a public room at an hour—between 3:15 and 4:00 P.M.—when it would be more or less deserted, and at others in a private one for which the prisoner was accustomed to make a small additional payment. Can it be doubted that there is some connection—possibly without the connivance or knowledge of either of these ladies—between this acquaintance and the place where the document was planted? Can it be reasonably doubted that the man this document was intended to benefit—the only individual in this country to whom it was worth a straw—the man who met the niece at Marlow—was the one who put it in the aunt's garden at Jordans?"

Jellipot had listened to the speech of the learned counsel with no sign of emotion, nor indeed of any very lively interest, until he came to this tea room allegation. It was, in fact, the first time he had heard anything with which he had not already known the prosecution to be familiar, and which he had not expected to hear.

But at this point he looked up sharply. He saw that Inspector Combridge had not slackened his efforts, and that his patient persistence had traced that which might easily have eluded a less pertinacious man. If he knew that, how much more might he have learned or guessed? But it seemed that Bullock had nothing further in that direction to say, and Jellipot sank to apparent inattention again as he went on to dilate upon the poetic impulses which appeared to be common to the murderer and Mr. Higgins, and to discuss that enigmatic line which had been rescued from the wastepaper basket of the hotel, until he wound up with a phrase of rhetoric, and began, one by one, to call the witnesses that his case required.

\* \* \* \* \* \* \*

The second day opened with Mr. Bullock well content. His witnesses were numerous, as is usual when a case is founded on circumstantial evidence, but their individual contributions were not lengthy, and were the shorter because Mr. Jellipot's interpositions were singularly few, and in several instances he did not cross-examine at all.

In this easy atmosphere, and in Bullock's able and experienced hands, the case built itself up in its cumulatively damning details, with little apparent effort from the defending solicitor to demolish or even delay the process.

Mr. Corder, observing this, felt mildly satisfied. He did not think it to be a strong case. But he thought it to be strong enough. He did not criticize Mr. Jellipot's apparent reluctance to develop a fighting front. He took it as confirmation of what he had already decided to be beyond reasonable doubt, that they had the right man in the dock; and when that is so, and the testimony against him is true, but somewhat less than complete, may it not be wise to remain silent till it can be considered as a whole, and the line of defense decided, without haste, or premature disclosure, in the interval that must divide committal from the trial itself?

Inspector Combridge, though somewhat less easy in mind, for he had learned before now that Mr. Jellipot might be most dangerous when his words were few, was not far from the same mind. Even Jellipot could not make bricks when the straw was nil. Besides, had he not been frank in saying that the case was too much for him?

Edward Higgins also was as content as a man can be who sees a net being woven around his life, and does not know that he will be able to break it through. After all, he thought, it was conjecture, and nothing more. It was guess—and guess—and he had heard already from that gross-jowled bounder who had seemed to take pleasure in insulting a man who could not reply, what the evidence was going to be. He only waited the time to come when he could go on the stand and deny everything, as Jellipot had promised that he should do.

Only the magistrates' clerk, Peascod, remembering his conversation with Jellipot, was a puzzled man. With a long experience of watching such legal battles he could observe the weak links in the chain, the witness who would be confused by a sharp assault, better even than the busy combatants would be able to do. And he thought that no half measures were possible here. If Mr. Jellipot intended, as he said, to ask that the defendant be discharged, he must first put him on the stand. Peascod could see no possible evasion of that, or how it would be possible for that to be done without the defense being completely disclosed. And if that were so, should not every weakness, every conjecture, in the case for the prosecution be relentlessly hammered out?

Yes even when Miss Le Noir, a plainly nervous woman, and one to whom truth was less familiar than lies, told her tale, Jellipot had let her go without a single challenging word. And Miss Le Noir's testimony, to Peascod's experienced and impartial mind, was of a quality that invited attack. It was absolutely without corroboration, and it was not given in a convincing manner. Why should it be believed that Emmoll had left at the hour she said? Even that he had left alive?

She said that he had had a meal at her house. But if that were false? Then the post-mortem evidence would place his death at midnight or little later than that. But Jellipot had listened, looked at her mildly, shaken his head when his turn had come, and silently let her go.

It was only twice that he had really stirred himself.

Once when the authenticity of the endorsement on the hotel bill had been discussed, and then his sole anxiety had appeared to be to get it clearly and emphatically upon the records of the court that it was Emmoll's handwriting, Emmoll's ink, Emmoll's receipted bill. In fact, that there could be no doubt that it had been written by him within a few hours of his death.

Well, that might, under some circumstances, be to his client's advantage. But it was also that on which the prosecution relied to bear down an otherwise trembling scale. And what use would its authenticity be to a hanged man? Still, Peascod reflected, there was the mother. It might mean that the money would go to her. Even murderers may not be destitute of some admirable filial instincts.

145

Suppose Higgins had recognized that his own position was hopeless, and had instructed his solicitor to concentrate on obtaining for his mother—to revenge whose wrong he had committed the crime—the wealth of the man he killed? That was possible in itself, but what then became of Jellipot's assertion that he should press for his client's discharge? Peascod pondered, and gave it up.

The other point which had roused Mr. Jellipot to unexpected activity had been the evidence of the foreman from Page's garage. The man's evidence-in-chief had been that the car, which had been ordered on the previous day, had been taken out by the prisoner at "about five o'clock. He couldn't say more exactly. The time hadn't been booked, as it had been hired by the day, not the hour, so that it was a matter of memory. But he had implied, in his uncertainty, that it might be later rather than earlier than the time he said. Still, the man was somewhat indefinite.

This time Mr. Jellipot rose to cross-examine in earnest.

"Mr. Binns," he said, "I am sure you desire to be a truthful witness?"

The man shuffled his feet as he replied uneasily: "Yes, I hope I do."

"I put it to you that you don't remember at all when that car was taken out? That you may not even have seen it go?"

"I said I wasn't sure of the exact time."

"In fact, it might have been—in fact it was—about 2:00 P.M.?"

"I should say it was after that."

"Why?"

The abrupt question reduced the man to a pause of disconcerted silence, which Jellipot broke by adding sharply: "Didn't you say five or later because that was what the police had suggested to you as more likely?"

"I didn't say it for that."

"But you got the idea from them?"

"I haven't said that."

"No—but I have. You won't swear that it wasn't two in the afternoon?"

"I've said that I'm not that sure."

Jellipot sat down, and Bullock, after a whispered word with Gayland-Jones, let the witness go. What did it matter? If Jellipot were content with scoring so small a point—well, let him! The case did not depend upon the time at which Higgins had taken the car.

# CHAPTER XVII.

MR. BULLOCK said that that was his case, and Mr. Elsworth looked at the clock. Mr. Jellipot's reticent demeanor had enabled the prosecution to present their witnesses in a more rapid succession than they had anticipated, and the time was still only 3.35 P.M. Mr. Elsworth looked at Mr. Jellipot. If he were prepared to say that his client reserved his defense, which seemed the most sensible thing for him to do, they could all go their several ways, and be home to tea. If he should say that he wished to open a defense for which he would not be ready till tomorrow, it would be no more than he was entitled to ask, after having been told that the prosecution would require the first two days, and it would be equally satisfactory in its immediate results, for lawyers, like the rest of the world, have no objection to a short day.

But Jellipot said neither of these things. He rose in his habitually diffident manner, and began to address the court.

"Before," he said, "I make my formal application for you, sir, to dismiss this case, I wish to explain my client's position, and there is some evidence which it will be necessary for me to call. But the time I shall occupy will not be long.

"Mr. Edward Higgins, as I need scarcely say after the evidence which the prosecution has put before you, is the son—the legitimate son—of the murdered man. That appears to me to be the sole and insufficient reason that he is in the position where he now stands.

"His defense is that his coming to this country had no connection whatever with his father's visit, and that he did not on any occasion see or communicate with him. He knows nothing whatever of his father's death, nor of the document on which the prosecution so largely relies. But he is naturally gratified—I may say that I am gratified on his behalf—that so much has been done in this court to establish that it is a genuine document, in his father's writing, and signed by him.

"His purpose in coming to this country was partly the accomplishment of a business deal, which he was empowered to negotiate at his own risk and expense, and in which, I am pleased to be able to say, he was successful. It was also partly—perhaps I should say primarily—to marry a young lady—Miss Prudence Manly—whom he had met in his own country, and to whom he is deeply attached—an attachment which is, I have reason to believe, equally reciprocated.

"His business was concluded about a fortnight ago, and when he had succeeded in that, and failed in his other object—for Miss Prudence Manly is not yet of sufficient age to marry without her parents' consent, for which he knew that it would be useless to ask—he booked his return passage.

"That is the innocent and absolute record of his visit to this country, which has had such a disconcerting termination. It is true that he hired a car for a few days, at a date which coincides with that of his father's murder, but he contends strenuously that that is not sufficient reason for charging him with so monstrous a crime. My instructions are that he considers that his occupation during those days is no one's business but his own, and his instructions to me are that he declines to give any explanation of what he did."

Mr. Jellipot paused a moment at this point, and looked round the court, as though to judge how this naive negative of defense was received.

Inspector Combridge had the relieved expression of a man who has been listening for the explosion of a possible bomb and finds it to be no more than a harmless squib.

The attentive gravity with which the magistrate listened did not change, but, with the last words, his eyebrows rose.

The prisoner moved impatiently. He was evidently restless, thinking that the moment for which he had been waiting had come, when he could assert on oath that which his solicitor was so haltingly stating on his behalf.

Bullock and his colleagues heard Jellipot with expressionless faces. They would wake to animation if he should show signs of having any damaging weapon within his grip, but it would have been discourtesy to an embarrassed colleague to show consciousness of the futility of the instructions that he was endeavouring to carry out. His was a puny argument.

Jellipot, observing how the declaration of his client's innocence was received, repeated more firmly: "Those are the instructions which I have from the defendant, but acting entirely on my own responsibility, there is a witness whom I think it is my duty to bring before you. I call Miss Prudence Manly."

"You mean," the magistrate asked, "that you wish Miss Manly recalled?"

"No. I call Miss Prudence Manly, the younger."

Jellipot looked round at the girl, who had risen with a pale, startled face, being evidently unprepared for the ordeal to which she was called. He beckoned her forward with an encouraging smile.

There came an angry, imperative voice from the dock: "Prudence, don't. Don't say anything! Leave it to me."

Jellipot turned back to the magistrate, with the fighting quality in his voice that a crisis brought. "I take," he said, "the entire responsibility for calling this witness."

Magistrate Elsworth plainly hesitated. It was an unprecedented position, and at such a moment it is not always easy to make an instant decision that subsequent judgment will approve.

"But if your client objects, Mr. Jellipot?"

"It appears to me to be of paramount importance that the truth should be disclosed before this case goes to a further stage."

Mr. Elsworth looked at the girl, still standing uncertainly in her place. "You are not obliged to give evidence, Miss Manly, unless you wish to do so, and especially not so if it would tend to incriminate you in any way."

The girl looked at her father, who had risen beside her. A word passed between them too low for those around to hear. She said in a firm voice: "Yes, I do," and made her way to the witness stand.

Having been sworn, Mr. Jellipot commenced her examination.

"I believe, Miss Prudence, that you are engaged to marry Mr. Edward Higgins, or Emmoll, as he should perhaps more properly be called?"

"Yes."

"It was without your parents' consent, and without their knowledge?"

"Yes."

"And had you asked for such consent, you knew that it would not have been given?"

"I knew Mother wouldn't."

"Do you know where Edward Higgins was during the afternoon of January 20$^{th}$, and the following night?"

"He was with me."

"Where?"

"We drove to Eastbourne in the car."

"To what address?"

"No. 3, Venice Terrace."

"And you stayed there?"

"Yes. Till Tuesday morning."

"Without your parents' knowledge?"

"Mother thought I was with some friends."

"But there would be people at Venice Terrace who knew you were there?"

"Yes. Several."

"Under what names did you stay?"

"Mr. and Mrs. Higgins."

"Mr. Higgins made no concealment of his own name?"

"No. Of course not. Why should he?"

"Why did you go to Eastbourne together?"

"To get married."

"But you found that impossible?"

"Yes, because I was underage, and because—that's how the laws are."

"So you can swear definitely that Edward Higgins did not have, and could not have had, any part in the murder of his father?"

"Yes. He couldn't possibly."

"Thank you."

Mr. Jellipot sat down. He was aware that he might have asked one or two further questions which would have placed this weekend adventure in a somewhat different light, but he saw also that the prosecution could not possibly let the girl's evidence go unchallenged, and he thought that those explanations might come out better in cross-examination than if he appeared to be prompting her to her own defense.

He had led her, frankly and clearly, and without excuse, to state the fact by which her lover's life could be saved from the peril in which he stood. Beyond that, let Bullock probe for what he would be less certain to find.

Bullock said: "Wait a moment, if you please, Miss Manly."

He spoke in his smoothest tone. In his heart he cursed all women witnesses, and particularly those whose black hair has a natural gloss, and whose lashes are long and curled over dark-blue eyes. Probably it was a whole or a partial lie. Perhaps a confusion of dates, to which a complaisant landlady would be persuaded to swear. Yet even so, he must move with caution, lest the law's prey should escape the net by a woman's wile. He rose slowly. Almost certainly the girl had perjured herself in a vain effort to save the murderer to whom she had lost her virginity, and whom, with a woman's perversity, she could still love, though she must know him for what he was. And the man had had the sense to see the futility of the lie she told, and would have held her back if he could!

That was the most probable guess, but it was less than sure, and he must hesitate on a road for which he was unprepared.

"You are quite sure of the date, Miss Manly?"

"Yes. Quite. Besides, Mother would know."

"You mean she would know you were away from home? She couldn't know more than that, could she?"

"That was what I meant."

"Was that the only occasion when you went away with Edward Higgins without your parents' knowledge?"

"Yes. Except when we met in the afternoons."

"You went away on this occasion thinking you could get married at once?"

"Yes. Edward knew we could in the States, and he thought it would be the same here."

"And you thought the same?"

"I didn't know differently."

"And although you were not actually married at the time, you booked rooms in the name of Mr. and Mrs. Higgins?"

"Yes. Edward—we thought it would save explaining anything—I mean any fuss."

"And when you found you couldn't get married, you will excuse me asking you, but it is necessary to be quite clear—but of course you occupied separate rooms?"

"Yes, of course."

Bullock smiled slightly. Whether the girl's tale were invention or partial truth, he felt that he had led her to that of which she might not see the significance till it was too late to recall, but which would destroy the value of the alibi she had been willing to sacrifice so much of her own reputation to build.

"Then," he said quietly, "you do not really know how Edward Higgins was occupied during the night?"

"I know we were talking together till after two."

The reply came so readily, and with so genuine a sound, that some of those who heard and had been most sceptical of this convenient alibi began to doubt what the truth might be.

Bullock shifted his ground.

"Can you tell me what makes you so sure that it was this week-end, and not the one before?"

"Well, it isn't so long ago that I should forget! It's only February now. Besides, it was then that we read in the papers that Mr. Emmoll was dead. It was on the day I went home."

"Wait a moment, Miss Manly, if you please."

Bullock had become conscious of a surrounding atmosphere of consultation. His legal colleagues were evidently desirous of discussing the position with him before he went further. He bent down to hear Ritchie say: "The girl's got her tale pat. It's either true, or she knows how to tell a good lie. It *was* on the Tuesday morning that it was first announced who Emmoll was. Why not adjourn now, and let the C.I.D. poke about a bit more. They ought to turn it inside out in a couple of days, and she's done for him, if it's a lie."

Bullock accepted this view. He straightened his back to say: "With the permission of the court, I should prefer to postpone the completion of the cross-examination of this witness for two or three days."

Magistrate Elsworth's face was inscrutable. "Any objection, Mr. Jellipot?"

"If the adjournment be for not more than a couple of days—"

"Then you do not wish to call other witnesses now?"

"No. I think not. But with your permission there is just one other question I should like to ask before Miss Prudence withdraws from the witness stand."

"Very well. I am sure Mr. Bullock will not object to that."

"You have told us, Miss Prudence, that you went to Eastbourne with Mr. Higgins in anticipation that you could get married there. When you learned your mistake, why did you stay until the following Tuesday?"

"Because—well, what else could I have done?"

"You mean you had nowhere else to go, unless you should have returned home before the date when you were expected?"

"Yes. I couldn't possibly have explained."

"And this anxiety to avoid bringing the position to the knowledge of your parents was paramount in your mind?"

"I didn't want—yes. I mean I didn't want to make trouble at home. It was no use saying anything. I knew Mother wouldn't agree—and we weren't married, and I had to go back."

"Very well. So you were at Eastbourne together until Tuesday morning. During that time would it have been possible for Mr. Higgins to have made long journeys without your knowledge?"

"No, it wouldn't. And besides, it's a silly idea."

"Why do you call it that?"

"Because—well, because we were thinking of other things!"

"This," Mr. Elsworth interposed, with a smile, "is becoming somewhat more than one question, Mr. Jellipot. I don't want you to lead the witness over the whole ground again."

"But with your permission there is still one point which it may be useful to make clear before the court adjourns. You heard, Miss Prudence, in the course of yesterday's evidence, a rhyme which I need not repeat, which was found with the clothes of the murdered man; and you heard subsequently that a line of verse which it was suggested had a rather ambiguous meaning had been found in the wastepaper basket of the room occupied by Mr. Higgins at Willing's Hotel. Had you seen that line previously?"

"Yes."

"How and when?"

"Before we went to Eastbourne. Mr. Higgins sent it to me."

"Would you oblige the court by repeating the context, so that its meaning may become clearer than it is now?"

The girl shot a swift glance at the angry man in the dock, and looked more uncomfortable than before. "I'd rather not, if you don't mind. They were nothing really. Only to me."

"I'm sorry, but I must press the question a little further." Jellipot looked down at a paper in his hand, on which it could be seen that there as a poem of considerable length. "Perhaps," he went on, "it may be sufficient if I read the following line only. This is what I have here:

*"Too faint the heart that in you lies the debt of life to dare,
For all the glory of your eyes, the splendour of your hair.*

"That is right, is it not?"

"Yes. Not quite. It's near enough."

Jellipot looked down at the paper again. "Yes," he admitted. "Not quite. I see that 'splendour' comes first. I am afraid I was trusting to memory as much as eyesight. Would you tell the court what you understood them to mean?"

"I should think anyone could see that. It meant that he wanted us to get married without anyone knowing. Without waiting till I was twenty-one."

Mr. Elsworth looked puzzled. "If that be the real meaning, Mr. Jellipot, it does not appear to me to be very clearly expressed."

But Mr. Jellipot, having ignored his client's earnest and explicit instructions, felt the greater obligation to defend him on other issues. "With due deference to that opinion," he replied firmly, "I must submit that the meaning is clearly there. I have thought myself that it is rather neatly put. And apart from my own reaction, I have made some inquiries into the subject, and am assured that, by modern standards, if these lines were condemned at all, it would be because their meaning is far too clear."

"That," Elsworth replied dryly, "I can quite believe. The case will stand adjourned until 10:30 A.M. on Friday next."

Jellipot turned to speak to his client. "I think," he said, "that you can rely upon your release on that day."

The answer was brief and pointed: *"You cad!"* The contemptuous words sounded clearly through the stir of the rising court and produced something of a shock.

Jellipot showed no sign of offense. "It is a point of view," he replied, "for which there is much to be said." He added inaudibly that there was something on the other side that he could not say.

Inspector Combridge met him as he went out. "You've been too much for us again," he said ruefully, "and how you do it I don't know."

"On the contrary—I can't expect you to understand—but the case has been rather too much for me."

He walked on, wondering whether, even in those enigmatic words, he had said too much. Inspector Combridge was no fool, as he had good reason to know. Still, he thought not.

As he came to the entrance, Mr. Manly was saying to his sister: "Yes, she had better go back with you. You'll know what to say to her, but I don't think she need worry. I mustn't stop to talk now. I want to get home, if I can, before Tabitha gets the evening paper."

He saw the solicitor as he spoke, and held out his hand.

"We haven't met before, Mr. Jellipot, but I must thank you for giving my daughter the opportunity of doing the right thing."

"Yes," Jellipot replied absently. "It's kind of you to say that. But I wasn't thinking of her."

# CHAPTER XVIII.

IT WAS on a morning towards the end of September, shortly before the law-courts reopened after the long vacation, that Mr. Jellipot entered his office with a copy of the *Morning Post* in his hand, and gave instructions for Chief Inspector Combridge to be called on the telephone.

When he heard his voice, he said: "I wonder whether you'd have time to call in this afternoon, say about three? I've got something to tell you about the Emmoll case that you'll be interested to hear."

The reply lacked enthusiasm. "I don't know that I shall. Not unless you're going to tell me who I can run in. I never want to hear Emmoll's name again, unless I can hear that."

"I'm not going to tell you of anyone you can run in. But I think you'll find that it will be worth while to come."

"Well, I'll be there."

The inspector's feeling had some excuse, for, among all concerned, he had been the one left without gain or credit of any kind in a case in which, as he told himself with some truth, he deserved less criticism than he had received.

To Edward Higgins it had brought a fortune, which he had been able to assume with his father's name. Beyond that, it had almost unbelievably smoothed the path to a marriage which had taken place within three weeks of the day when he had stepped out of the dock, his name cleared by the testimony not only of Prudence Manly, but of half a dozen Eastbourne witnesses who had proved the impossibility of his having been engaged in nefarious activities eighty miles away.

For Tabitha Manly had taken the news of her daughter's amorous escapade in a surprising manner. The misguided girl, having forgotten her duty to her Creator and to her earthly parents, and all the precepts of modest conduct which had been taught from her earliest years, had now no alternative but to marry the man with whom she had been associated in so shameless a manner if, of course, he were still willing; which, somewhat to Mrs. Manly's expressed surprise, it appeared that he most emphatically was.

Inspector Combridge appeared punctually at Jellipot's office. Though he had a lively curiosity concerning that which he had been invited to bear, he could not avoid a preliminary reference to the loss which the legal world had suffered by the untimely end of Denis Hartlin, K.C., the news of which had been in the morning papers.

"It's a bad business about Hartlin," he began; "everyone's saying that he'd have been Attorney-General in the autumn if Trisk has to go."

"Yes," Jellipot replied. "I believe that was understood, and I don't think there could have been a better choice."

Denis Hartlin had been on a motoring holiday in the Tyrolese Alps. The previous afternoon his car had swerved to avoid collision with a cyclist—had skidded—struck the parapet of the road—broken through it—and crashed on the pine tree tops seven hundred feet below. Denis Hartlin had been instantly killed, and his chauffeur, Blake, had died in the following hour.

Jellipot went to his private safe. He took out an envelope, heavily sealed. He said: "It is owing to Mr. Hartlin's death that I have asked you here to receive a document which he entrusted to me against such an eventuality. You will see that it is directed in such a way that it would have gone back to him had he outlived me, as would have been the more probable course of events."

"I have always thought," Inspector Combridge said—and spoke no more than the truth—"that he had more to do with that matter than ever came out, though what it was I couldn't see; and to have suggested it after the mess I'd made—! I suppose you're not going to tell me that he killed Emmoll himself?"

"Not precisely. But why should you speak of it—after having formed the sound opinion that he had something to do with it—as though that were an impossible thing?"

"Because it was. I don't say there couldn't have been any circumstances in which he would have killed anyone. I don't think there are many of whom you'd say that for sure. And he told me himself that he thought Emmoll was better dead than alive. But he wouldn't have dealt with him in that brutal way. Hartlin wasn't the sort. You know that as well as I."

"Yes. I know that. But that—and I'm afraid it was my own suggestion to him, though it was not seriously made, that led to it being done—that was why he did it in that way. Actually, Emmoll killed himself, but Hartlin was responsible for his death."

"You always said it wasn't a one-man job."

"That was evident. But Blake helped him from first to last."

"And you knew this all the time?"

"No. I guessed it at first, and then, when Higgins came on the scene, I didn't know what to think."

"And Hartlin would have let Higgins be tried for something he hadn't done?"

"No. That was the worst trouble I had. It was when I went to ask Hartlin to take the brief for Higgins that I first heard the truth. He asked me to dine with him at the Savoy, and in a private room there he told me the whole tale. He had decided to inform Scotland Yard at once, and would have done so on the previous day, but Blake was almost as much involved as himself, and he had to be sure that he felt the same.

"The fact was that they had taken precautions against almost everything else, but they hadn't considered the possibility of anyone being in serious danger of being convicted of the crime. When Hartlin saw the mess Higgins was in—and how the way he had acted himself had the effect of throwing suspicion upon him, though of course that hadn't been meant—he thought he ought not to lose a minute, at whatever cost, in getting an innocent man free.

160

"I must have argued with him for two hours that night, and then again with Blake down at the car. I told them there would be time to do that if I failed to get Higgins off. But the most I could get was a promise that they would wait over the Tuesday, to see whether he would be committed.

"That was the mess I was in, and I don't think I ever had a worse weekend. I knew that the only chance of avoiding a committal was to put Prudence Manly on the stand, and I had spent all Friday afternoon arguing with Higgins, who wouldn't agree that she should be called.

"In the end, I decided to call her, even against my client's instructions. I don't say it was right or wrong, but—to have seen a brilliant and most useful career ended in such a way—to have seen misery and shame brought upon innocent and happy people (there wasn't only Hartlin's family, Blake had one as well)—and all because I was dealing with three obstinate men! Others might look at it differently. They might regard my scruples as antisocial, and particularly so in an officer of the court, but when I thought of the consequences, all of which I could avert by putting that young woman on the stand—well, it was too much for me!"

Inspector Combridge made no comment upon this candid statement of Jellipot's sentimental weakness. He said: "Well, I suppose it's all here, but I must say it's about the most incredible thing I ever heard. When I think of the way the body was stuck up, and that verse about having done it when he was drunk, and—"

The inspector stopped as though obstructed by the incredibility of his own thoughts, and Jellipot answered his half-articulated astonishment.

"I can easily understand how it appears, but the whole idea was to do everything in such a way that everyone would know that Mr. Hartlin would have done it differently.

"This idea, as I may have said, is one for which I was originally responsible, in conversation with Mr. Hartlin; but I could not reasonably have anticipated that he would have adopted it as he did. But bizarre as some of the features of the crime certainly were, I understand that the actual murder was contrived in an extremely simple and natural manner.

"The plan having been agreed with the chauffeur, who was evidently loyal to Hartlin, Emmoll was invited to dine at the Savoy. At the end of the meal, after he had, so to speak, pleaded guilty to the murder of Hartlin's cousin, Hartlin, showing no great resentment at so long-past an incident, mentioned that he was going down to Devon for the weekend, and offered to run Emmoll to Southampton, which would be little, if at all, out of his way.

"Emmoll excused himself at first, on the ground of the call which he said he must make in Marsden Terrace. Hartlin had to offer to pick him up after that, and also invent a rather ingenious reason for asking him not to mention to Miss Le Noir that he would be travelling in Hartlin's car.

"It also made the difference that everything was some hours later than it had been planned, and delayed the disposal of the body till the following night.

"But, after they picked Emmoll up, everything appears to have gone smoothly enough. Emmoll knew little of English roads. They might have driven him into Norfolk or Gloucestershire before his suspicions would have been aroused. Besides that, he was soon asleep. He was a tired man.

"Hartlin had decided upon the Loudwater house because he remembered, from the time he had gone over it with the agent, how solitary it was and how thickly wooded on every side.

"But more particularly he remembered having noticed that the French window of the dining-room would not fasten properly, so that he anticipated getting in without difficulty, as in fact they did.

"Before that, he had relieved the sleeping man of the gun which, even in this country, it was Emmoll's custom to carry. And when Emmoll was waked by the car pulling up at the drive, he found himself being invited to get out, with a gun-barrel poking unpleasantly into his spine.

"I suppose," Mr. Jellipot speculated, "it must have given him a home-from-home sort of feeling in this effete country to be greeted in such a virile manner; but when he realized that they were two to one, beside being armed, he did what he was told, and gave no trouble at all.

"You'll find Hartlin says he told him straight that he hadn't many minutes to live, but if he behaved quietly he would be allowed to cut his own throat, instead of being executed in a much more painful manner; and as a further condition he was to write that he was about to end his own life—which was true enough—and mention the worst thing he had ever done as a reason for that suicide.

"Well, we know what he wrote. It mayn't have been just what Hartlin expected to get, but it is probable that Emmoll, realizing that his last hour had come, felt a genuine inclination to right the wrong he had done both to his son and his lawful wife. Anyway, so it was. And when they had got that from him, they tied him by one leg to the grate, and then Blake told him the time had come, and offered him his own knife. So he really did cut his own throat—under persuasion, of course—though Blake was frank enough to say that he might have given his elbow a jerk at the right moment, as Emmoll didn't seem to realize adequately how far the knife ought to go in to make a reasonably quick job.

"After that they spent so much time in removing all traces of their own presence—they had to do it all by the light of a portable lamp they had brought—that when it was finished they decided it was too late to attempt to dispose of the body, and that it would be less risky to take it back with them. A natural decision and a wise one.

"Blake was the only one, besides Hartlin himself, who had access to the garage, and the rooms behind and over it where he lived. No one would be likely to be searching for Emmoll's body. No one had any reason to expect that there had been any murder at all. And if the evidences of the crime had been found earlier than they were, and even if any sign of Hartlin being there had been overlooked—actually you did find a tire mark the car had made—there was the obvious explanation that he had looked over the property. So Blake set to work at leisure to finish the matter in such a way that it would be evident that Hartlin couldn't have done it—and therefore hadn't.

"I believe Blake was the author of that six-lined stanza with the distressingly redundant adverb, that set you looking for all the drunken lunatics on the records of Scotland Yard."

Inspector Combridge heard this explanation in a frowning silence. He sat without attempting to open the written statement in which these events were formally get out over the signatures of the two men who had conspired to commit the crime. He considered the audacious method by which he and his department had been outwitted, the germ of which had come from Mr. Jellipot's too-fertile imagination, and he could not be expected to feel pleased.

He felt puzzled also—so much so that he still had a doubt of whether he were being fobbed off with a partial tale.

"Well," he said at last, "if Hartlin says that's how it was, and you say he's right—! But there are some things that still seem a bit queer to me. How he picked Jordans for putting the body the way he did, and then you, who'd given him the idea, being there that night! You must see it's a bit thick."

"You mean that it has the look of an extremely improbable coincidence? So it does. It had puzzled me. But Hartlin explained it very simply. I had mentioned to him a few days before that I should be visiting a client there during the weekend, and this brought it to his mind, and then he thought what a whimsically incongruous place it would be to choose. Indeed, I'm not sure that the character of the village didn't inspire the idea of the unseemly way in which the body was exhibited.

"As a matter of fact," Jellipot reflected, "if coincidences, so-called, be examined with sufficient care, it will be found that the great majority of them are not properly such at all, but are the result of a logical probability not apparent to a more careless regard."

"I dare say they are," the inspector replied indifferently. "But there's one thing you haven't mentioned that beats me to understand by logical probabilities or anything else. That's the question of how that paper got into Miss Manly's grounds, if Higgins didn't have any hand in the game."

"But the explanation of that," Jellipot replied, "is so simple, so natural, that I should have thought it could be deduced without the redundancy of explanation being required.

"When Denis Hartlin considered the substance of the confession which the hotel-bill bore, he saw that it was a document which might be of essential value to those whom it directly concerned, and he felt no obligation to deliver it to them. Need I say that he was anxious to do it in such a way that his own part in the matter would not appear?

"Actuated by these conflicting motives, he cabled a firm of trustworthy inquiry agents in New York for information respecting Lucille Higgins and her son.

"These agents obtained some particulars, among them being that Edward Higgins was said to be engaged to an Englishwoman named Prudence Manly This was an item of information which they naturally thought to be of importance, in view of the inquiry they received having come from this country.

"But the information they sent, probably owing to the cautious manner in which they had been instructed to obtain it, was incomplete. They did not send the girl's address. Neither did they learn that Edward Higgins had come here.

"Denis Hartlin saw, as he thought, a method of passing on the document which would be safe for himself and consistent with the maniac method by which he had disguised the authorship of the crime. He made a direct search for a name which was not likely to be duplicated, and found a set of telephone directories to be sufficient to give him what he required.

"But for Edward Higgins' unfortunate presence in this country—itself a quite natural thing, for he was simply fulfilling the masculine habit of pursuing the girl he loved—the event should have been satisfactory in its result. And even had it tended to suggest a connection between Emmoll's death and his betrayal of Lucille Higgins in earlier years, the effect could only have been to divert suspicion to a mistaken and which would have been an abortive, direction.

"Had Hartlin been able to make his inquiries more openly, he would doubtless have been more fully and accurately informed, and would not have made the blunders he did. Had he been less conscientious, he would have put the document on the fire, rather than hazard the consequences of attempting to pass it on to those whom it concerned.

"And so," Mr. Jellipot concluded reflectively, "the moral appears to be that murder, unless under the most urgent necessity, should not be committed by a too-scrupulous man."

# ABOUT THE AUTHOR

SYDNEY FOWLER WRIGHT (1874-1965) penned over seventy volumes of science fiction, fantasy, classic mysteries, historical novels, poetry, and non-fiction, many of them being published by the Borgo Press Imprint of Wildside Press.

www.ingramcontent.com/pod-product-compliance
Lightning Source LLC
Chambersburg PA
CBHW020645180626
46816CB00003B/1124